The Devil Wears Baccarat

Jatoria C.

The Devil Wears Baccarat

Copyright © 2024 by Jatoria C.

All rights reserved.

Published in the United States of America.

All rights reserved. No part of this publication may be reproduced, distributed, or transmitted in any form or by any means, including photocopying, recording, or other electronic or mechanical methods, without the prior written permission of the publisher, except in the case of brief quotations embodied in critical reviews and certain other noncommercial uses permitted by copyright law. For permission requests, please contact: www.colehartsignature.com

This is a work of fiction. Names, characters, places, and incidents either are the products of the author's imagination or are used fictitiously. Any resemblance of actual persons, living or dead, businesses, companies, events, or locales is entirely coincidental. The publisher does not have any control and does not assume any responsibility for author or third-party websites or their content.

The unauthorized reproduction or distribution of this copyrighted work is a crime punishable by law. No part of the book may be scanned, uploaded to or downloaded from file sharing sites, or distributed in any other way via the Internet or any other means, electronic, or print, without the publisher's permission. Criminal copyright infringement, including infringement without monetary gain, is investigated by the FBI and is punishable by up to five years in federal prison and a fine of $250,000 (www.fbi.gov/ipr/).

This book is licensed for your personal enjoyment only. Thank you for respecting the author's work.

Published by Cole Hart Signature, LLC.

Mailing List

To stay up to date on new releases, plus get information on contests, sneak peeks, and more,

Go To The Website Below...

www.colehartsignature.com

Too much lightness will burn and too much darkness will destroy. But if the right darkness alchemizes with the right lightness, the two combine to create a beautiful disaster. - Jatoria C

Dear Readers:

If you are familiar with my work, then you know you are in for a wild ride. The book you are about to read is a DARK interracial romance book. Some of the triggers included are profanity, graphic violence, dub/non con, explicit sexual situations, forced proximity, and kinks such as bondage, impact play, and sex toys.

This book is a work of fiction and none of the material mentioned should be performed without proper research done.

The Devil Wears Baccarat Playlist:

1. Neoni- Darkside
2. SAYGRACE-You don't own me
3. Michel Plasson- Lakme Act 1
4. Sabrina Claudio-Unravel me
5. Julia Michaels- Heaven
6. T-pain- Put it down
7. Kehlani-Gangsta
8. Teddy Swims-Lose Control
9. Rihanna-Kiss it better
10. Sza-Snoo

Alexandur

"Betrayal makes my ass itch."

"If your ass is itching that means it is dirty, brother. May I suggest a warm shower with soap?" my youngest brother Roman replied. My eyes flew to his face. Roman stared back at me with his cold chestnut brown eyes and blank face. My father called Roman the mystery because his face rarely showed any emotion. It was hard to tell what he was thinking and even harder to try to guess what his actions would be.

"I would have to agree," a deep voice said in a matter-of-fact tone. There was no point in me looking back to where my big brother Constantin stood. He would not spare me a glance back anyway. Constantin was too busy running through every scenario in his head for problems known and unknown. He was a genius with an IQ of 150 the last time he checked. That was the reason my father called him the mind.

"Just kill me, you fucking monster," a weak, feeble male voice mumbled. My eyes went to the last voice in the room. The man was chained down to a black chair and savagely beaten. He was a scrawny, tall man with blond hair that covered half of his face. From the angle of his nose and the swelling of his jaw, I would assume that a few of my earlier punches had caused some of the bones in his face to sprain or crack. Slowly, a smirk appeared on my face. Killing always brought me an indescribable feeling of peace and happiness. My father took me on my first kill at the age of twelve, and from that moment I knew what I was meant to be in this life. My father expected me to be afraid that day but instead, I took his knife and created art using human blood and bones. Ironically, my first kill was in the same building we stood in now at the back of my parents' house. My brothers and I liked to refer to it as our kill room, but it was big enough that it could easily be converted into a two or three-bedroom condominium. Our father is the "Nasu," which means the godfather in Romanian. He often joked that both God and the Devil blessed him because he was given three sons who each possessed a unique quality that was needed to rule with an iron fist. Individually we were a threat, but together we were unstoppable. The mind, the mystery, and the monster were one hell of a combination. I do not know if God would bless the ruler of the Romanian Mafia, but I keep my thoughts to myself. Pondering if serial killers were allowed to live peacefully in the afterlife was not a concern of mine. I am who I am, and I accept that.

"Were we not good to you, Zack?" I asked the chained-up man as I walked over to the table where one of our soldiers had the tools I requested. As I looked down at the different knives and drills, an image of how I would arrange Zack's dead body appeared in my head. The anticipation of creating such a masterpiece had me wanting to rush the process, but patience was a virtue. I picked up a simple scalpel and turned back around to the traitor to look at him while he stuttered out bullshit.

"I did not have a choice. They threatened to kill my daughter," he cried.

"Save the tears, you are in for a long night, my friend. You have been working for our family for six years. You knew how to come to us if there was a threat. Now, thanks to you, not only do we have two shipments missing but one of our highest-ranking soldiers was found dead this morning."

Zack did not respond but his cries got louder. Zack came from an extensive line of criminal intellects. His father used to be our main tech guy and he trained Zack to take over as soon as he graduated from college. Zack knew what was required of him and the consequences for if he fucked up. For the last couple of months, strange shit had been happening. It started when my father got a call that the shipment of cocaine for La Cosa Nostra did not make it to Sicily. That did not make any sense to me because I personally got on our private jet and flew from Atlanta to New York to oversee the shipment. Growing up, my father would always tell us stories to teach us lessons. One of those lessons was to always be involved in everything attached to our name and to never trust the people under us to oversee important business. This lesson was drilled into our heads because my grandfather was betrayed by a person he trusted his life with. Sixty-seven years ago, my grandfather had to take his wife and kids and flee Romania. At the time he was the Nasu, but his right-hand man had betrayed him and set him up for the murder of a high-ranking government official. Like all bosses, my grandfather owned local and federal politia and was good friends with a couple of them. My father said he used to always tell him the importance of networking and having good bonds with the people you network with. My grandfather was not supposed to be friendly with the politia he paid under the table to handle his dirty work, but he would invite a few of them over for family events and outings. One night he received a phone call after midnight from a politia that he had become good friends with and was informed his fingerprints were all over a crime scene and weapon. The gentleman who had been murdered was not only a high-ranking government official, but he was the son of the police chief. The police chief planned to raid my grandfather's house the next morning and have him arrested. The plans were supposed to be kept quiet because they knew that would be the only way to catch my grandfather. The politia involved knew there would be a shoot-out and bloodshed during the arrest, but if they kept their mouth shut the risk could be minimized. After my grandfather got off the phone, he had to make a quick decision. He had more than enough money to fight the allegations, but he was blindsided by the murder. The killing was not a sanctioned kill and if he had done it, they would have never found any evidence linking him to the crime. If he stayed and fought the allegations they would keep in him prison until trial out of fear of retaliation. My grandfather was the most feared man in Romanian, and he knew that even in prison he would be protected to a certain extent. Romanian prison was a hell hole, and the inmates were subjected to mental and physical abuse daily. He decided the best thing to do was to gather his family and leave the only place he knew until he could figure out what the hell happened. My grandfather ended up coming to the United States to New York City. It was his first time ever being in the United States, but it was the obvious choice for the head of the Mafia. Although cities such as Chicago and Baltimore had heavy Mafia presence, it was nothing compared to New York. New York was the home of five different Mafia families until my grandfather came over and made it six. My grandfather fell in love with the fast-paced city and only returned to Romania once after he found out who had double-crossed him. He flew in undetected overnight and killed his former right-hand man and his whole family and then flew right back out nine hours later to New York City. A couple of years later he opened his own wine company called the Bucur Wine International Company and used his influence and connections to turn it into one of the largest wine companies in the world. The Bucur Wine International Company now produces about five percent of the world's wine, which is roughly twenty-three billion bottles annually. We now had companies in all major cities including Atlanta, where we decided to relocate twelve years ago and take over because Atlanta was one of the highest-earning cities in the United States and at that time did not have any heavy Mafia presence. The majority of our wine is only shipped overseas because it is easier for us to smuggle drugs and guns using our own boats. The boat that left the harbor that day had the drugs under the wine in bubble wrap like we do all over our shipments. I checked each box of wine myself and confirmed that the amount being shipped out was correct. When we first got the news, my father thought the Coast Guard had betrayed us. My father paid the Coast Guard to look the other way and after he called them upset, we found out they had nothing to do with the missing shipment. They provided us with video evidence that our boat sailed the ocean untouched by them. If the drugs were not confiscated by the Coast Guard, that meant the shipment had to be taken once it hit the island. The La Cosa Nostra made it clear that they had nothing to do with the missing drugs and we believed them. Our partnership with them dated back over a century. They were one of our closest allies and our families are friends. The drugs on that damn boat were worth sixty million dollars that we had to replace and then fly out to Sicily and meet with the family there to show our respect and apology for the fuck up. The next month the same shit happened; this time the shipment was set for Colombia. It was not until this morning when one of our highest-ranking soldiers was killed at his home that we realized we had a rat problem. Initially, we assumed it was one of the other Mafia families trying to stir up trouble secretly so they could barge in and take over Atlanta, but it still left the question of how they got such privileged information. We only sent out one shipment a month and the day and location were always different. The Mafia is stuck in their ways about a galore of things including who we used to get information for us. We did as all the other families did and chose one of the criminal intellects who was raised to work for the Mafia. Unfortunately for us, the criminal intellect we chose betrayed us, and betrayal must be handled accordingly.

 I leaned down and used the scalpel to cut a small line on Zack's cheek just to watch the blood drizzle down his face a little, before using the same scalpel and plunging it into the right side of his hip. Zack screamed out in pain, and it sounded like opera to my ears. Opera music was relaxing to me and if I were alone, it would be playing softly in the background. I pulled the scalpel out of his right hip and plunged it into the left side of his hip. The scalpel was small, and the puncture wound would not kill him nor cause him to bleed to death. The hip was one of the worst parts of the body to get injured or stabbed in and the sounds coming from Zack's mouth proved that he was indeed in pain.

What a pussy! All rats deserve to die a slow, painful death for opening their big fucking mouths.

"Calm down. Sadly, today is not the day you will die."

Zack's whimpers got quieter, and he looked at me with hope in his eyes.

Silly, silly boy.

"Who paid you to betray us, Zack?"

The hope quickly faded out of his eyes and fear made a reappearance. Slowly, he shook his head left to right to let me know he would not say. I grabbed a handful of Zack's hair and pulled his head back. My face lowered until we were only a few inches apart and staring each other in the eyes. I wanted him to see the monster inside of me that was craving to come out.

"Please just kill me, I cannot tell you. You do not know what they promised to do to my daughter. I must protect my child," Zack whispered.

You already failed at protecting her. You put your own child in the path of a monster and assumed she would remain untouched.

Small drips of blood were still falling down his face. I stuck my tongue out and licked up a few drops before standing up. When I was back standing at my full six-three height, I turned around to put the scalpel back down and picked up some masking tape. It only took me a minute to tape Zack's mouth shut.

"I will go bring it in," Roman stated. I nodded my head in confirmation and walked past Zack to grab another chair to place in front of him. Zack's face was frowned up in confusion when I placed the empty chair in front of him, but I could not understand the incomprehensible words coming from his mouth.

"For some odd reason, people seem to believe that women and

children are off-limits and would be safe from harm. Those kinds of people are not very smart people. You graduated at the top of your class, so I assumed you were not like those types of people. I apologize for my misassumption."

Zack's eyes got big and clouded with tears. Behind me, I could hear the kill room door opening back up. Tom was the head of our family security and had been standing outside the door with the package as instructed. My brother walked up to me with a plain brown box in his hand and handed it to me. I opened the box and lifted Zack's daughter's head out of it and placed it down on the chair in front of him. When I sliced her head off her eyes were still open and that is how I left them. Zack was now crying profusely and fighting to get out of the chains. Eventually, he would tire himself out. For the rest of the night, he had no choice but to stare into the eyes of his dead child and realize the importance of keeping his fucking mouth shut. After me and my brothers exited the kill room and locked the door, I handed the empty box back to Tom. When we got here Mama was in the kitchen cooking and I could not wait to clean up so I could eat.

An hour later my brothers and I had all showered and changed. There was not much blood on my clothes but that did not stop me from burning them to ashes. I could have gotten Tom or one of the other security guards to do it, but my father taught us to always clean up our own messes and to only trust each other with our freedom. Now we all sat at the dinner table eating the cabbage rolls my mother had prepared for us.

"I plan to take care of Zack's father tonight," our father informed us. Our father was in his sixties but looked much younger. His pale beige skin was clear of any blemishes. He was a big man, the same height as me, who worked out regularly. My brothers and I had inherited his emotionless chestnut brown eyes. The only major difference between us was that his hair was brown, and we all had black hair like our mama.

"Are you sure? We can handle it," Constatin asked him.

Constatin was our father's second-in-command and would one day be the Nasu. Roman and I were considered Capos.

My father lifted his head and glared at him. He hated being questioned and we knew not to say anything else on the topic. Father rarely got his hands dirty because there was not a need for him to when he had us, but I guess this offense was too personal not to handle.

"After his father is handled, we must find a new tech person. Are we going to borrow one from another family?" Roman asked all of us.

When we grabbed Zack, we took his laptop with us hoping it would provide some clues on who was trying to attack us, but Zack had some security system protection encrypted on it that required professional help to crack.

"No, I do not think it's a good idea to let outsiders know that we are under attack until we know more. Let me think more on it. I will have a solution by the time we leave work tomorrow,," Constatin replied.

Father made sure that not only were all of us on the board of Bucur Wine International Company, but all three of us were over a department within the company. Constatin was over the financial accounting department, Roman was over the human resources department, and I was over the Protective Service Department. Monday through Friday I worked at the company during the day and then got off and did whatever my father needed me to do for the Mafia.

"No more shop talk. I made a delicious Albinita," Mama said softly. All three of us nodded our heads in agreement. Father was a ruthless man, but Mama was the sweetest woman I know. She rarely raised her voice and always had a smile on her face. Most wealthy families hired housekeepers and cooks, but Mama refused to. She cooked every one of our meals and spent her younger days running behind three extremely active little boys. She was patient with us and showered us with love every day. I will never forget the first time I saw Mama get mad. It was the day we had gotten expelled from primary school. This little boy had been picking on Roman because Roman was quiet and stayed to himself. Constatin found out about it and questioned Roman. Roman admitted it was true that the little boy had even gone as far as stealing his lunch box from him. Constatin was furious and told Roman he should have beaten the little fucker up, but Roman feared getting in trouble with father. Constatin told him that his respect was more important than a verbal lashing. The next morning, instead of us going to our separate classes, Constatin and I followed Roman to his class. Roman did not ask us why we were following him, probably already expecting a change in events. Roman walked into his class and over to this desk where this little boy sat talking to his friends. Roman did not say one word, he just cocked back and punched the boy dead in his nose. The little boy was shocked and tried to fight back but it was useless. Roman was pounding on the little boy's face repeatedly. The whole class was in an uproar. The teacher ran over to where we were to try to break it up, but we pushed her back. Roman said she knew about the bullying and did nothing. She should have done her job when it was time, now it was too late. Upset, she ran out of the room yelling for security. One of the security guards came running in the classroom and I kicked the fucker in his balls. Two more security guards came running into the room and we tried fighting them all off, but they quickly snatched us up and carried all three of us out of the classroom. The principal was livid. The little boy my brother beat up needed medical attention and was sent to the hospital. The principal told us we deserved to go to juvenile jail for the way we acted but because our father donated so much money to the school, they would not press charges. The primary school we were attending was full of rich snobs and I knew the real reason he would not press charges was because he was afraid. I thought that fear would have him calling Mama instead of Father to come get us, but I was wrong. Thirty minutes later, Father and his two security guards stormed into the principal's office. The principal suddenly appeared apologetic when he told Father what we had done. He explained that because of the severity of our actions, he had no choice but to expel us or he would lose his job. Father was so mad he was red the whole ride home. He told us we should have waited to beat the boy up after school and promised us a good lashing when we got home. I think I was only like eight or nine at the time and we had never got a whooping before. When we got home Father was still yelling. He pulled his belt off and told us to pull our pants down and turn around. Roman yelled out for Mama while doing as Father said. Mama came running down the stairs. When she saw Father with the belt in his hand, she went off. Father was trying to explain what we did but Mama did not care. That was the only time I had ever seen Mama raise her voice. She told him if he put his hands on us, she would leave him. He told her he would kill her before he let her leave. Mama stood her ground and said she was going to pack up all her belongings and we would be gone by nightfall. Father threw the belt on the floor and went chasing behind her. They argued for hours but in the end, Mama won. Father never raised his hand to hit us again. Instead, he would find other ways to punish us. He would make us run laps with bricks in our hands or do two hundred push-ups with weights on our backs. There was not a person in this world that I loved more than my mama, and most of the time when she asked something of me I did it with no hesitation.

I enjoyed dinner with my family for another hour before we kissed them both goodbye. Me and my brothers stopped back by the kill room to check on Zack. He was no longer fighting the chains as I expected. Instead, he was crying silently with his eyes closed. Taunting a broken man was beneath me so I did not waste any words on him before closing the door back. My parents' house was built like a fortress, and they always had at least four security guards on the premises. It would take an army to take them down and even more to take out my parents. Even with that knowledge, we still checked the premises before walking around to the front of their mansion. All of us stayed on the outskirts of Atlanta in Kingswood within twenty minutes of each other.

"Don't be late to work," Constatin stated as I hit the open button on my key fob to my all-black Bugatti La Voiture Noire. Without responding, I slid inside my car and sped out of the driveway.

Every morning, I got up at five a.m. to work out in my gym before taking a shower and heading to work. This morning was no different. At exactly 7:45 I parked my car into my designated spot in the private employee parking lot of Bucur Wine International. Regular employees had another parking lot to use. This parking lot was only for the top executives of the company. Both parking lots were guarded heavily but this parking lot could only be accessed with a passcode and retinal verification. Bucur Wine International was located in Buckhead in downtown Atlanta. It was the best area for business but because of the heavy traffic, security was a top priority. Today was Friday, which meant I had to evaluate the new security guards that were recently selected on proper protocol. It was the last step of the hiring process, and each new hire had to pass both the physical and written test with one hundred percent accuracy or they were escorted off the premises. Slowly, I got out of my car and waited for Tree and Hero to fall in step behind me. Both of my security guards stayed with me and followed me everywhere I went unless I directed otherwise. Tree and Hero have been my security guards for twelve years, ever since my sixteenth birthday. If it were up to me, I would not have security guards at all, but unfortunately, the Nasu made it clear that the security guards were nonnegotiable. Our whole family's security was provided by the same team of mercenaries and Tom, my father's main security guard, was over the selection of our security detail. Tree and Hero were good at staying in the background and only making their presence known when necessary. I would not say we were friends because I didn't have friends, but they were close associates. They respected my wishes and we rarely got into disagreements. One of the few disagreements we did get into was them wanting to drive me around all day. That was not happening nor were they getting in the car with me. Now they followed behind me in their own vehicle whenever I had to go to work or an event. If I am with my brothers, we normally do not take security unless we plan on being around a lot of people.

It took us almost the whole fifteen minutes to make it to the top floor of the facility where my office was located.

"Good morning, sir," my secretary Mrs. Martin spoke as soon as I stepped off the elevator. She was an elderly white woman with long gray hair that she kept twisted up in a bun in the back of her head. Mrs. Martin had been my secretary for the last two years and we worked together perfectly. The majority of the time she did not bother me, and I have never had a problem with my schedule or her completing a task. The secretary I had before her was a younger woman. She was beautiful but aggravating. Every time I turned around, she was finding reasons to come into my office to ask ridiculous questions. If only she knew the number of times I imagined slicing her tongue off with one of my knives, she would not have been so quick to be in my personal space. By the end of the third week of her working for me, I had my mind made up that she had to die. Unfortunately, the next day when I came to work, she was gone, and Mrs. Martin was there in her place. Mrs. Martin informed me that Constatin had hired her to take over and handed me a coffee cup. Without saying a word, I sipped on the coffee and let the taste simmer on my tongue and down my throat. Mrs. Martin had not only stopped at a local coffee shop right down the street that in my opinion sold the best coffee in Atlanta, but she also got me a black coffee with two espresso shots the way I liked it. I gave her a head nod and that was the beginning of our harmonious work relationship.

"Good morning, has one of my brothers been by?" I asked her while picking up the coffee she was holding out to me.

"Yes, Constatin stuck his head in your office a little over five minutes ago," she replied while typing something on the computer. Constatin was a stickler for being on time, so I was not surprised by her response.

"Okay," I replied before walking to my office door. When I made it to the office door, I stopped and moved to the side to let Tree and Hero search my office.

"All clear," Tree said five minutes later before they both got the fuck out of my way and out of my eyesight.

The rest of the workday passed by quickly. Training and testing days were my favorite. I took the company security seriously because I believed if we were attacked the attackers would assume the best place to attack us would be at work. They would assume wrong, but that's usually how assumptions go. An hour before it was time to go, I was heading back upstairs to my office to add the security guards who passed both exams onto the computer.

"Your brother is waiting on you in your office," Mrs. Martin said when I made it to my floor. I nodded my head in response and continued walking to my office. When I opened my office door, Constatin was standing looking out of the electrochromic glass windows at the busy downtown Atlanta area. I entered my office and walked over to my desk to have a seat. He people watched for a couple of minutes longer before he turned around to speak.

"Brother, I know you planned on having fun tonight, but I need you to rush to finish the project."

I do not want to rush killing. Killing is an art and should be done in a masterful way!

"Are we doing more than one project tonight?"

"No, not in the way you want. Tonight, we are going to get the new computer geek."

"That does not sound like it should be complicated. Why can I not take my time on my project?"

"The new computer geek might take some persuasion, but he has something of value that we can use."

Hmmm, so we are going to force somebody new to work for the family. Interesting.

"I will handle the project in a swift manner," I replied and gave my brother a small smile. Constatin smiled back before walking around my desk and out of my office. Something inside of me told me tonight was going to be a wild night, and I loved wild nights.

The rest of the workday went by quickly. Anticipation had my mouth watering randomly every time I imagined my blade slicing into Zack's throat. If only time was on my side, I would have cut and sliced to my heart's desire. At exactly five p.m., I was walking out of my office and to the elevator. Tree and Hero followed me out of the office building and to my parents' home. When we reached my parents' gate, they watched me pull in before driving away. They knew not to expect me back home until later tonight. Whenever they did not have to follow behind me, they had the freedom to do as they pleased. I did not allow strangers in my home so if they wanted to see any family or friends, then they did so while I was with my family. By the time I pulled into my driveway tonight both would be there waiting. On most nights I would not have anything of importance to inform them of so I would relieve them of their duties for the rest of the night. Their rooms were located on the east wing of my home, and I respected their privacy, so I hardly went over to that side.

Both of my brothers' cars were already parked in front of our parents' home. I parked beside Roman's car and got out. My mama was probably in the sitting room waiting for me to come in, but I had murder on my mind. Instead of walking through the house and out the back door, I walked around the house and straight to the kill room. Tom gave me a slight head nod as I opened the kill room door. It was silent in the room. Both of my brothers stood looking at Zack with bored expressions on their faces. Zack was still chained down, his eyes now fixated on his dead daughter's head. He had to hear me enter the room, but he did not look up at me.

"Zack, you have no idea how excited I am to see you today. Did you have a good night?"

Silence was my only answer. He did not even blink his eyes. I walked over to my tools and picked up a hunting knife with a serrated blade on the end of it.

"Who paid you to betray us? Tell me the truth and I will make this quick and painless."

Seconds passed before I realized he still had no plans to talk. A mixture of disappointment and understanding hit me at the same time. Zack had accepted his fate and decided to continue his oath of silence. If only he had kept his oath of silence to the family, I would not be pulling his head back slightly and positioning my knife on the side of his neck. Slowly, I cut him from ear to ear, making sure to slice his arteries and trachea in the process. Blood oozed out of his neck and onto my arm. I inhaled the scent, letting it flow through my veins. Blood had a metallic smell to it, but death had a darker, intoxicating scent. A scent to which I was addicted. By damaging the arteries in his neck, blood flow to his brain was compromised. Within one minute Zack lost consciousness. A few more minutes later he was dead.

"Come on brother, let's go dispose of his body," Constantin stated. I stood to my full height and gave him a quick head nod. The disposal of his body took us about an hour. Once his body was disposed of correctly, I took a shower and put on another suit. Still in a daze from the kill, I glided down the stairs after I had gotten dressed to find my brothers. They both were in the sitting room.

"Where is Mama?" I asked them.

"She retired early. She has a headache," Roman replied. I made a mental note in my head to go check on her before I left while taking a seat on the chaise.

"What is the plan, brother?" I asked Constantin and then listened closely as he replied.

Kenya

"The girls are counting their tips and cleaning up to get out of here," Chris stuck his head in my office to tell me. It was a little after eleven at night and I was exhausted. Hooters was always busy at nighttime, but Friday and Saturday were a madhouse.

"Thank you, tell the girls I will be right out to help them," I replied. Chris winked his right eye at me before walking away from my office door. Chris was one of our bartenders and fine as fuck. He was tall, dark chocolate, and had a head full of dreads. He had high cheekbones, big lips, and hazel eyes that glowed whenever you peered into them. He was used to the women he encountered falling at his feet. I think that was one of the reasons why he still flirted with me even though I turned him down nicely every time. Men always want what they cannot have. Chris has had a crush on me from the first day I started working here as a server. At the time I was not single, and two years ago when I became single my desire to date again was nonexistent. Maybe in another lifetime I would have given him a chance, even if it was just to have a little fun, but I had responsibilities that didn't include wasting my time for something I knew wouldn't go anywhere. I quickly finished entering the end-of-the-day data into the computer before shutting the computer down. When I exited my office, I made sure to lock my office door before rushing back to the front to help the girls get out of here. As a former Hooters girl, I knew how tired the girls were and I helped them out as much as I could.

Forty-five minutes later, I was locking the restaurant up. Chris was standing outside the door like he did every night when he worked, but I do not know why. He knows I have my gun license and I carry my Ruger SR22 everywhere I go.

"I'm off tomorrow, boss lady, but I can come up here before closing to make sure you make it to your car safely."

"Do not be ridiculous, I am fine. You know I know how to shoot first and ask questions later. Plus, I know you have a million things better to do than to worry about me on a Saturday night. You are only twenty-one, you should be out having fun not worrying about your boss."

"You say that like you are not only one year older than me. I know you got a lot on your plate, Kenya; I just want to lighten the load."

Not only was he fine as fuck but he was smooth with his words.

"I appreciate the thought, Chris. You are so kind and a good man. You will make some young woman happy one day, but that woman isn't me."

"Mannnnnnnnn, you gon' say yes one of these days, and when you do…"

Chris had lowered his voice to make the words coming out of his mouth sound sexier, but it was a wasted effort. I do not know if my ex-boyfriend broke something in me that made it where I no longer desired men or if it was just life in general. Either way, I cannot remember the last time I was turned on by anybody. We reached my white 2018 Nissan Versa, and I quickly scanned my car for any signs of a break in. Car burglary is a major issue in Atlanta. My car had been broken into twice, both times during work hours, and the police did not find any leads or the items I had stolen. I hit the unlock button on my key fob to unlock my car doors. Chris reached out to open my driver's door for me and I gave him a quick smile.

"Thank you, Chris. You are such a good friend. I appreciate everything you do. When you get married, I am going to dance at your wedding," I replied while accentuating my country voice. I was born in a small town in Alabama. My family did not move to Atlanta until a few days after my fourteenth birthday.

Chris burst out laughing before waving me off. He closed my car door, and I watched him walk to his car and get in before I took my gun out of my purse and placed it in the glove department. After I closed the glove department, I put my seat belt on, cranked my car up, and then pulled out of Hooters' parking lot.

The drive home took about twenty minutes because I lived on the north side of Atlanta. My two-bedroom home was not much, but I was lucky to find a place in what I considered a somewhat safer part of Atlanta. The neighborhood I lived in had a lower crime rate compared to all the other neighborhoods I searched through when I went looking for a home. When I pulled into the parking lot, I was not surprised to see my little brother's car parked in the driveway. Kofi was eighteen and mostly a loner. I encouraged him to go out and have fun with the few friends he had on the weekend, but it rarely happened. He took our parents' death hard and for a while he completely shut down, only doing his schoolwork and sleeping his days away. It took a year and some expensive ass therapy to get him somewhat back to his normal self. Kofi was better now, and he was happy, but he was no longer the innocent child who looked at the world with wonder. I believe when people lose somebody close to them it changes them, and that person they were before no longer exists. One day we were one happy family and the next I was told to go to the office to speak to the chancellor. I remember the confusion I felt on the way to the chancellor's office. I was only in my second semester at Clark University and my grades were good. Unlike most college kids I was not out partying every weekend or making new friends. Me and my high school boyfriend Keith both decided our senior year of high school to attend the same college so when I was not studying, I was spending time with him. Now that I look back, I wish I would have gone to parties or had more fun because after I had a seat at the desk in my chancellor's office, my whole life changed. The chancellor informed me that my parents had been gunned down at a stoplight and they both were dead. Everything after that moment happened so fast. I had to plan for a double funeral and call the family members we had in Alabama. There was no way I was letting my little brother go back to Alabama with family members we barely talked to and he damn sure was not going into the foster system. I was appointed guardian over him and given a twenty-five-thousand-dollar insurance check, as if that could fill the hole I had in my heart. Foolishly, I thought I could continue school and manage the adult responsibilities that were thrust in my face. For the first six months after our parents were killed, I would get up and go to college and use the insurance money to pay the bills, pay for therapy, and pay for my brother's private school. After six months the money was almost gone, and I had to make some tough decisions. I dropped out of college and got a job at Hooters. The tips I made were generous and it was enough to keep a roof over our heads and my brother in private school. Kofi wanted me to unenroll him from the private school, but I was not hearing it. My parents moved from Alabama to Atlanta for two reasons. One was because my father found a job with the city that paid more than what he was currently making. The other reason was because my brother was approved as a scholarship kid to one of the hardest private schools to get in, in the United States. Because he was a scholarship kid my parents only had to pay five hundred a month for his classes and another five hundred for his meals. I would have worked a hundred hours a week if that meant my little brother could continue attending private school because he was a genius and deserved to be where he could learn. He graduates from private school next month and he had offers from all the Ivy League colleges such as Princeton and Yale. He turned them down though to attend MIT. He was going for a degree in computation and cognition. I cut off my car and grabbed my stuff before slowly getting out. The walk from the driveway to the house was small and within a few minutes, I was inside my home. The smell of food hit my nostrils and my stomach growled. I locked my front door and walked upstairs to where my and Kofi's rooms were. The sound of the TV playing let me know that Kofi was awake. When I reached his room door, I knocked on it softly a few times and waited.

"Come in," Kofi yelled out. I walked inside his bedroom and smiled. Kofi was sitting at this computer working on something with anime playing on the TV in the background. His room was small, but he had pictures of all his favorite anime characters on the wall.

"What are you doing?"

"I got frustrated earlier playing the game and decided that I could make a better game than the one I was playing."

I chuckled softly before wrapping my arms around him from the back and giving him a small hug. It was not until I hugged him that he stopped typing on his computer to look up at me.

"In the refrigerator are turkey burgers and a salad. All you have to do is warm it up to eat."

"Thank you for cooking, Kofi. You know I could have made me something quick when I got here."

"You would not have though. You would have taken your shower, eaten something small like popcorn, and then went to bed."

You are right but I am not admitting it.

"And here I thought I was the one who was supposed to be taking care of you," I replied while laughing.

"You take good care of me, which is why I help whenever I can."

"Thank you, Kofi. I am exhausted. I am about to shower and

then eat. Breakfast will be ready by the time you wake up in the morning."

Kofi had already started back typing so instead of verbally replying, he just nodded his head. I wrapped my arms around him one more time to give him a quick hug before walking out of his room. Like clockwork, the feeling of guilt hit me as I made my way to my bedroom to grab what I needed to take my shower. In a perfect world, I would be home every night at a decent time so I could eat dinner with my brother or have a fun night out on the town. He was basically raising himself and I felt like no matter what I did, it wouldn't make up for all the time I spent at work.

Girl, stop it! You are doing the best you can and that is all that matters.

I wanted to argue with the know-it-all voice inside of my head, but I was just too tired. Forty-five minutes later I had showered, eaten, and was now in my bed. Briefly, I debated if I wanted to turn on the TV to watch a show before I fell asleep, but my eyelids were barely staying open. The last thing I remember thinking was if I would make turkey bacon or sausage in the morning for breakfast before the darkness took over and I drifted off to sleep.

I do not know how many hours had passed before I felt someone tapping on my shoulder.

"Kofi, if I open my eyes, my left foot is going to go so far up your ass it is going to come out of your right ear," I fussed at my brother without opening my eyes or rolling over to see what he wanted.

"You know that's not possible, right," a deep voice with a weird accent replied.

What the fuck? God, if I open my eyes and somebody is trying to rob me, it is about to be some slow singing and flower bringing!

Tap. Tap. Tap. Whoever was in my bedroom tapped on my shoulder again. Pissed, I rolled around off my stomach and onto my back. Slowly, I opened my eyes. Standing around my bed were three men all dressed in black suits.

"God, I don't know if this is some kind of joke or test, but if you made the devil and his fallen angels this fine you need your ass whooped," I said aloud before closing my eyes to go back to sleep. I do not know what kind of dream I was having that felt so real, but there was not a way in hell those fine-ass men were really inside my bedroom. Those men looked foreign, rich, and in the wrong damn house.

"If your brother's life means so little to you then by all means, please enjoy your rest," another voice with an accent spoke. Quickly, I sat up in the bed and opened my eyes back up. It was still dark outside of my window, so I stared at the three men for a couple of minutes hoping they would disappear or something while my vision adjusted completely. After a couple of minutes, it was clear that I was not dreaming, and these three men had really broken into my home.

"Where is my brother?" I asked them.

"Downstairs," one of the men replied. He stood in the middle of the three men and if I had to guess, all three men were related. All three of them had similar features. Light, tanned skin, dark eyes, small lips, and black hair. They had all to be over six feet tall and they were all of the same ethnicity. The one in the middle that just spoke looked like the oldest. He had a superior air about him that gave off he was the boss. The one on my left had to be the youngest. His blank face had a youthful appearance to it. My eyes went to the one on the right and I froze. All of them had chestnut brown eyes, but his eyes were so dark they looked black. The smell of danger and something expensive and familiar flooded my senses. Nothing was ordinary about the men standing in my bedroom. I joked about God sending the devil and his fallen angels into my bedroom, but it looked like the joke was on me. Regular danger was something to which I was accustomed. Regular danger was something I could handle. These men were not regular danger though. The man on my right stared back at me and a fear like I have never known wrecked my body. The man staring back at me was not just dangerous, he was something far more sinister. My right hand went under my pillow and wrapped around my gun. I got a good grip on it and let my trigger finger slide on top of the trigger without applying pressure to it. I counted to three in my head and without hesitation, I lifted my gun from under my pillow and pointed at the man on my right.

Alexandur

Kenya, Kenya, Kenya. I repeated her name in my head while staring at the woman in front of me. She had skin the color of dark chocolate. Her lips were juicy and plump. Her nose was straight with high cheekbones. Her hair was covered with some kind of big cloth, and she had on a black spaghetti-strapped shirt. Kenya was beautiful, but it was not her beauty that had me staring at her so intently. It was her eyes. Even in the dark I could see the anger building inside of them. She was pissed that we were inside her bedroom. I expected her anger but only after her fear. Kenya did not show fear though. She took her time looking over each one of us without saying anything. When she looked in my eyes, her big brown eyes widened slightly. In that moment, I realized she saw the monster inside of me. Over the years, my brothers have told me that when I turned deadly, my eyes changed. They said my eyes turned darker and so intense that anybody looking at them would know I was trouble. In this particular moment though, I wasn't in a deadly mood. If anything, I was still feeling a high from killing Zack and was quite relaxed.

How in the hell did she see the monster I had tucked inside of me?

After Kenya's eyes widened slightly, I saw when she slid her hand under her pillow. If I had not been watching her so intently, I would have missed it, because she did it so smoothly. Even with me watching her, I still only had a few seconds to pull my gun from my waist before I saw the black chrome coming from under her pillow. We both lifted our guns up and at each other at the same time. Constatin mentioned he had done a background check on both Kenya and Kofi, and other than their parents' murder he did not find anything alarming. If I had not known that, I would have assumed that little Miss Kenya was a killer. She held her gun steady in her hands without trembling. If we had been in the room by ourselves, I had no doubt in my mind that she would have pulled the trigger.

"Both of you put the guns down. Kenya, if you shoot my brother, we will kill both you and your brother, and that is not what we are here for," Roman said. Surprisingly, his voice was not bland as usual but instead, he sounded entertained. Kenya was quiet for a moment before she looked away from me and to my younger brother. Another moment passed before she nodded her head and then handed her gun out to Constatin for him to grab it.

Not only is she beautiful and fearless, but she is also smart enough to figure out Constatin is the boss. Hmmmm.

My dick swelled a little inside my pants and I had to mentally threaten him not to get all the way hard.

"Is my brother really alive?" she asked Constatin, and I could finally hear some fear in her voice.

"Yes, he is tied up downstairs. If you could pack some clothes up and come downstairs, I can explain the situation better to you. We are not here to kill, but to hire," he replied.

"That's funny, because I am pretty sure neither one of us applied to work with a group of psychopaths, but yet here y'all are," she replied before rolling her eyes. This time her voice had more of a southern twang to it.

Kenya got out of bed and walked toward her closet. My eyes

followed behind her as she walked. She had on a matching pair of black shorts that showed off the round shape of her ass.

"Can I change in peace, or should I just start stripping?"

My dick jumped at the thought of seeing her naked, but the idea of my brothers seeing her naked at the same time had me ready to bash their faces in.

"We will be right outside the door. Do not be stupid or your brother will pay for your stupidity. Make it quick," I replied harshly before either one of my brothers could speak. I turned around and walked out of Kenya's bedroom, knowing my brothers would follow. As expected, they followed behind me. Constatin waited until her bedroom door was closed before he questioned me in a hushed tone.

"What is wrong with you, brother?"

"Nothing is wrong with me, but I think it would be best for Kenya and Kofi to stay with me. You can come over in the afternoon and train him there. By the end of the day tomorrow I will have everything a computer geek needs to find the answers we seek."

"You know I do not like changing plans at the last minute. You are acting strange. There is nothing wrong with them staying with me as we previously discussed."

"You cannot watch over them as good as I can. You have more responsibility on your plate as the second in charge."

"Bullshit. We all have two security guards on our premises at all times. Why do you want them to stay with you? Hell, we are only twenty minutes away from each other. You can come over to my house to make sure I am safe while they are there if that is really your concern."

"It is not about them, it's about her. Brother finds her interesting and I do not know if that is a good thing. He will end up fucking or killing her. Knowing him, it would probably be both," Roman finally added his opinion to the conversation.

"I won't kill either one of them," I growled out.

Kenya opened her bedroom door, ending our conversation.

She looked over each one of us before shrugging her shoulders as if she could tell we had been arguing, but it was none of her business. In her hands was a pink suitcase and over her shoulder was a black bag. How she packed so much stuff in a matter of minutes was a mystery, but we had bigger things to worry about. Constatin started walking toward the stairs and we all followed behind him. The walk downstairs was a short one. Her whole house was the size of one of my guest bedrooms. When we made it to the kitchen, her brother was still tied up to the chair we put him in at the kitchen table. On his mouth was the tape we had placed there to keep him quiet while we woke Kenya. He was given the same opportunity to pack some clothes up as his sister had. He brought two suitcases down the stairs and his school book bag. All of it was sitting beside him on the floor. Kenya took one look at him and ran to where he was. She snatched the tape from his mouth, and he groaned slightly.

"Calm down, Kenya. Your brother is fine. Get up and have a seat at the table so we can talk," Constatin ordered. Slowly, she stood up and did what he asked but not before looking at my brother with murder in her eyes.

"First, I would like to apologize for the late intrusion. Time is of the essence. I am Constatin. My brother here is Roman and my brother there is Alexandur. It seems we have found ourselves in a sticky situation, but Kofi, we believe you can help us figure everything out."

"Is that why y'all are here, because you need my help?" Kofi asked Constatin.

"Yes, we need a new tech guy, and you have the job. You start your first assignment tomorrow after school. The assignment is simple. I have a laptop that I need to bypass the security system protection to figure out who is targeting my family. The security system protection was placed on the computer by someone highly intelligent and I assume it will take you a few weeks to crack. If you crack it, congratulations, you will become our permanent tech guy, and if you fail, well, it was nice knowing you."

Kofi's eyes got big, and he looked at us in shock.

"Who the fuck are you guys?" Kenya asked angrily.

"Well, to most people we are just equal owners of Bucur Wine International. A company my grandfather started many years ago. To other more dangerous people, we are the sons of the Nasu."

"What's a Nasu?" Kofi asked.

"Nasu means the word godfather in Romanian. That is what they call my father because he is the godfather of the Romanian Mafia."

"Wait, wait, wait. Let me get this straight. You motherfuckers are the Mafia and instead of hiring some rich-ass smart kid to do your dirty work for you, you plan to kidnap us so Kofi can do it?"

Kenya's voice was full of disbelief as she questioned my brother.

"Precisely. You see, the Mafia is stuck in their ways. One of those ways is that each family has their own tech guy to find information. We tend to follow the tradition and hire the person who has been raised to take over the position but unfortunately, that is no longer an option. He was a rat and now he is no longer among the living. Now we need to find out who paid him to rat and that is where you two come into play. Really, it is a great opportunity. If he finds out the information we need, we will deposit a million dollars into his bank account. At that time, we will discuss his future pay and what will be required of him. I must inform you though, that this position is permanent, and it passes down from father to son for generations."

"Shit, y'all might as well kill us now. My brother is NOT getting involved with that crazy ass shit. Who in their right mind would agree to some bullshit like that? So not only does he have to risk his life to work for your family forever, but his kids have to follow in the same footsteps. It is a hell and a NO. The only thing I ask is that you shoot me first. Kofi is the only close family I have left, and I do not want to see him die."

Constatin shrugged his shoulders and went to pull his gun from his pants. My heart started speeding up and for the first time in my life, I contemplated pulling my gun out on my own brother.

"Stop. Please, stop! Do not shoot my sister. She is overprotective of me, and I love her for it, but the decision is mine to make. I accept the offer, only if you agree not to separate us and to deposit another million in Kenya's bank account once I complete my first assignment," Kofi's voice rang out.

Slowly, a smile appeared across my face. Kofi might only be eighteen, but he was already a smart businessman. We never planned to separate the two anyway. People tend to listen more when they are trying to protect a loved one from getting hurt. My brother put his gun back into his pants and nodded his head in agreement.

"You two will be staying with my brother. We are aware of school and work, and we want you two to continue with your daily activities as normal. A guard will always be with you two when you are not at my brother's home, but the guard will stay in the shadows to keep suspicion down. I will come over in the afternoon or nighttime to see what all you know Kofi and what I need to teach you. Everything should run smoothly if you both remember the number one rule. Never, ever tell anybody you work for the Mafia."

Kenya scoffed before shaking her head.

"Which one of your brothers will we be staying with?" Kenya asked.

"Alexandur," Constantin replied and pointed at me. I sent him a thank you with my eyes before turning my head back to look at the kitchen table.

Kenya's eyes met mine and we stared at one another for a few moments before she opened her mouth to speak again.

"Why can't we stay with you or the other brother? No disrespect, but it is easy to see his elevator don't go all the way to the top."

Roman burst out laughing, causing me and Constatin to look at him in shock.

"I like her, brother. She is going to be the death of you," Roman stated after he finished laughing.

I hadn't the slightest clue what Kenya meant with her statement, but I knew it was some kind of insult. Regardless of if she wanted to stay with me or not, she was going.

Instead of replying to my brother, I pulled my knife out and walked over to Kofi. I cut the rope we had tied on his hands and feet and set him free.

"Grab your shit and let's go. I am ready for bed," I told them and walked toward the front door.

Kenya

The ride was silent with only soft opera music playing in the background. Occasionally, I would sneak peeks at my brother, but I was not ready to talk to him yet. I knew he made the best decision back at the house, but I do not think he understands just how deep in bed he was putting himself with the fucking Mafia. In all honesty, I know the main reason he agreed was that he did not want them to kill us, but I fear there may be a part inside of him that craved the danger we were entangling ourselves in. Death was the only other choice, and I was not afraid of dying. From the moment a person is born, death is the only guarantee you get. Everybody dies one day and there is nothing anybody can do to change it. Perhaps my parents' death left me more morbid than I realized. Either way, the decision had been made and now we just had to survive this the best way we could.

Dorothy, we are definitely a long way from Kansas, was my only thought as we pulled into Alexandur's mansion. His mansion was big enough to fit at least four regular-sized homes inside it. His grass was cut to perfection and the perfect shade of moss green. His bushes were trimmed down and shaped in a cute circular design. On his porch were two statues of angels. Both angels had their heads down and wore a cloak. In their hand was a scythe. It was both comforting and creepy to look at. Alexandur pulled in front of his mansion and parked. He hit the button to cut his car off and got out. Kofi got out next and then walked around to the right passenger side door where I still sat and opened the door.

"Thank you," I mumbled.

"You're welcome," he replied. His voice was slightly hesitant, and I hated that. I reached out and wrapped my arms around him to give him a quick hug. Regardless of whether I agreed with his decision or not, I never wanted him to question my loyalty to him. Alexandur had watched the whole exchange with a frown on his face.

The people who stayed in Atlanta were not as big on manners as Alabamians are. They were not rude, but they kept the pleasantness to a minimum. Kofi and I were raised to always use our manners and to show southern hospitality. Alexandur walked to his front door and pulled his keys out of his suit pocket. *If his body looked like that in a suit, I could just imagine what he looked like naked.*

Quickly, I shook my head to clear my brain of such silly thoughts. Alexandur should be the last man on earth I was having freaky thoughts about. He had what the old people called "crazy eyes." All three of the brothers were clearly comfortable taking people's lives, but Alexandur had something inside of him that was pitch black. After Alexandur unlocked his front door, standing in the doorway were two men. One of them was tall with black hair that swooped in front of his face. The other was a few inches shorter with blond hair and a cut on his face. Both were very handsome men.

"Is everything okay, boss?" the one with the blond hair asked Alexandur.

"Yes, this is Kofi and Kenya. They are friends of the family. Starting tomorrow, Hero you will escort Kofi to his high school and watch over him in the background until school gets out. He is to be brought right back here unless otherwise directed. Tree, the same applies to you. Tomorrow morning, take Kenya to her job and watch over her carefully. I don't need to tell you two what will happen if anything goes wrong."

"No problem, but if we both are occupied who is going to watch over you?" the tall one he called Tree asked.

"Nobody."

His reply was quick and harsh. Alexandur was a cold-hearted man.

"Your father isn't going to like that," the one he called Hero mumbled. Alexandur looked at him with his "crazy eyes" and Hero dropped his head.

Hell naw, this motherfucking man is insaneeeeee. All I need him to do is show me where my cell block is, and he will not have to worry about me.

"Can you two bring their luggage out of the truck? Their rooms will be right beside mine. After that, y'all are dismissed for the night. I will see you both in the morning."

Tree and Hero nodded their heads in agreement as Alexandur hit a button on his car key fob.

"Excuse us, ma'am," Tree stated. I moved to the side so that they could walk around us and out the front door.

"Come on, they will bring y'all stuff upstairs. My bedroom is on the west wing. You two will take the rooms right beside mine. All the rooms have a fully functional bathroom inside of them and a walk-in closet. Tomorrow, I will show you all where the theater and the gym are. My guards stay in the east wing and neither one of you should be over there unless it is an emergency."

For some reason, when he said that last sentence, he looked at me. Did he think I was some kind of whore or something? I mean, his bodyguards were good looking, but dating was the furthest thing from my mind. Alexandur walked down the long corridor that led to the stairs. As we followed behind him, I took my time looking at my surroundings. His walls only had one family picture on them, the rest were gods and goddesses from ancient mythology. We passed by two rooms filled with furniture, so I assumed one was his living room and the other a family room. The kitchen was the next room we walked past and my fingers tingled with excitement. His kitchen was so big that I could only see half of it, but what I did see was a chef's dream come true. It was full of high-end appliances that I could not wait to use. When we neared the stairs, my eyes almost popped out of their sockets. The staircase split into two parts separating the west wing of the house from the east wing. They were created like stairs from ancient Rome or Greece.

When Alexandur made it to the top of the stairs, he took a left toward the west wing, which led us to another long ass hallway. This hallway was full of what I assumed was only bathrooms and bedrooms. We only walked past two rooms before he stopped and opened the door on the right.

"This room will be yours, Kofi," he said.

"Thank you," Kofi replied before walking inside of the room. Alexandur walked down two more rooms and then opened another door.

"This room will be yours, Kenya. Obviously, my room is the one in between both of y'alls. Everything you need should already be inside, but if not, just let me know and I will get it."

"Thank you."

I had to speak quickly because he had already turned around and walked back toward his bedroom. Slowly, I walked inside of my new room for the time being and took a deep, deep breath. Just a few hours ago, I was leaving work like any other day, and now I was standing inside a room that cost more than anything I have ever owned times ten. My head started throbbing, signaling the approach of a headache. In the corner of the room was a long white couch. I walked over to it and had a seat. I needed to calm down so that I would not work myself up too much. How do I stay calm, though, when my world had just got turned upside down again for the third time in my life? A knock at the door interrupted my thoughts.

"Come in."

Tree opened the bedroom door and brought my luggage inside.

"Thank you, sir."

"No problem. I will be up early in the morning to take you to work. If you need me before that, just ask the boss and he will show you where our rooms are located."

I doubt that. He made it very clear to stay the hell from over there.

"I will," I replied instead of saying what I was really thinking. Tree smiled before walking back out of the room. I decided to spend a few more seconds in despair before getting up and unpacking my belongings. Briefly, I debated on going to check on Kofi, but I knew he was busy putting his stuff away. One of the first items he received when he started private school was a free MacBook and he loved the hell out of that laptop. After he finished putting his clothes away, he would spend the rest of the night on that laptop searching for all the information he could find on the Bucur family. I decided I had spent enough time freaking out, so I got up and walked over to my suitcase. Half an hour later I realized Alexandur was right when he said anything I needed probably was already in the room. The closet had empty hangers hanging up on the clothes rack. The bathroom was equipped with every basic hygiene product a person would need. Inside the closet in the bathroom there was a stack of fresh white rags and towels.

After everything I brought was organized, I took a shower. It was almost two in the morning when I finally crawled into my new bed. I had to be back up at six in the morning to get ready for work so as soon as I closed my eyes, I fell asleep.

ALEXANDUR

Ninety-eight. Ninety-nine. One hundred. I held the weight bar straight up in the air for a moment before placing it back on the weight rack. My chest heaved up and down while sweat dripped all over my body. I could not sleep well last night. My thoughts were filled with one certain woman, and I don't know why. The only explanation I could come up with was that it had been a few weeks since I laid with a woman, and I needed to release a lot of pent-up energy. That was why I went so hard in the gym this morning. I ran an extra two miles on the treadmill and did three extra sets of reps on the weights. My gym was equipped with a sauna and shower room. At least three times a week I would sit in the sauna, but today I bypassed it and walked right to the shower. While I showered my thoughts went back to Kenya. What was it about her? She was a beautiful woman, but I was used to beautiful women. I had never slept with a Black woman before and maybe that's what made her so intriguing. Either way, I wanted her out of my mind. I had more important things to concentrate on than a woman I just met. At exactly six fifteen I was dressed and walking down the stairs. The smell of something delicious cooking invaded my senses. My stride increased as I made my way to the kitchen. Tree and Hero never cooked breakfast. The most I had seen them do was warm up takeout. As I approached my kitchen entrance, the sound of laughter made me pause for a moment before walking inside it. At the kitchen table sat Kenya, Kofi, Tree, and Hero. They all talked among each other while eating. Kenya must have sensed my arrival though, because whatever Tree said that put a smile on her face was quickly replaced.

"Good morning, Alexandur. I made everyone a spinach and feta omelet with some cut-up fruit. Would you like one? It will only take me a few minutes to make."

I stared at the woman, confused. Last night she was feisty with a smart mouth and this morning she was offering to fix me breakfast. If everybody wasn't already eating, I would think she planned to poison me. I nodded my head in response and walked over to my built-in espresso machine. I could hear Kenya behind me opening the refrigerator and the sound of eggs cracking.

"You know, cooking is not something you have to do. If you want to then by all means, but I can hire a chef to make our meals if that is what you prefer."

I really did not like the idea of hiring a stranger to do anything for me, but the words were out of my mouth before I could stop them.

"If it is okay with you, I prefer to cook. Breakfast is the only meal I can guarantee I have time to make for Kofi. Most nights by the time I get home he has already eaten. Plus, I'm a southern gal and I enjoy cooking."

"Okay," I replied before sipping my black coffee. When I turned around Kenya was at the stove making the omelet. Her hair was not covered up anymore. Instead, her long black hair was in some kind of curly style.

What time did this woman get up this morning? I wondered as I had a seat at the kitchen table. Kofi looked at me and gave me a head nod. I returned the gesture. He and the bodyguards were discussing some new game that was coming out. In all my twenty-eight years of living, I have never played any game system, so I tuned the conversation out and watched Kenya. She flipped my omelet in the air while softly humming. My stomach growled and I frowned. Breakfast was not something I consumed on a regular, I just did not have the time. I do not know what I expected to happen this morning, but this was not it. Why were they taking being kidnapped and forced to work for the Mafia so easily? Suspicion clouded my mind. A couple of minutes went by before Kenya approached me with a plate. On it was the omelet, cut-up strawberries, and blueberries.

"Do you always eat like this?" I asked Kenya. She waited until she was sitting back down to answer me.

"If you mean do I always eat healthy, then the answer is yes. I am careful of the food items I place in my mouth."

"Is there a reason?"

"Yes, the reason is I like to eat healthy."

Ahhh, there goes the smart mouth.

"Why are y'all so happy this morning? Whatever you two have planned, I would advise against it."

"Nobody is planning anything. We just are not the type of people to walk around with a stick up our asses. Shit happens all the time that we cannot control. That is life."

She shrugged her shoulders and looked away from me to join back into the conversation with the others.

With my fork, I cautiously cut a small piece of the omelet and put it into my mouth. Surprisingly, it was as delicious as it smelled. No wonder the bodyguards were smiling and laughing. Without saying another word, I finished eating the rest of my breakfast.

"I'm out. Have a good day," Kofi said to his sister before reaching out to give her a fist pound. He stood up and carried his plate to the sink to wash it. There was a brand-new, state-of-the-art dishwasher right there, but he didn't even glance at it. At this point, I was thoroughly confused. Nothing went as I expected this morning, and I did not like it. I watched Kofi and Hero leave before Kenya stood up and did the same as her brother.

"Give me one second to grab my purse and phone. I will be right back," she told Tree before rushing out the kitchen and toward the stairs.

"What do you think of them?" I asked him as soon as she was out of earshot.

"Kofi seems like a good kid, and he is really smart. Kenya is nice. We tried to turn down the offer for breakfast, but she was not hearing it. Not to mention the woman is beautiful to look at."

"There are a lot of beautiful things to look at in this world. For instance, the next time I catch you looking at her, I will be admiring the beauty of your eyeball in my palm."

Tree's mouth dropped open and his face turned ashy white. Kenya came rushing back into the kitchen ending our conversation, but there really was not anything left to say. Two minutes later, they both were leaving at of the house. If everything continued going smoothly eventually, they would get their own cars back but for now, they had to prove they could be trusted.

Work was uneventful. As usual, Mrs. Martin had my cup of black coffee with two espresso shots waiting for me. After drinking two cups of coffee back-to-back, I craved danger. The last kill was not enough to satisfy the monster inside of me for long. Being in the Mafia was not like it was portrayed in the movies. The higher up you were the less you had to get your hands dirty. In Atlanta alone we had about twenty-five high-ranking soldiers that we could call for any problem. Those soldiers had other low-level soldiers under them. In all, there were about one hundred fifty of us scattered throughout Atlanta. The only time my family got involved with frivolous activities was when we considered the disrespect to be intolerable, which made it personal. When things got personal, we made sure to leave an impression that usually involved killing multiple people as a lesson. Other than that, it was necessary to keep a low profile and move smart. Right before lunch, I had a knock at my office door and then my brothers walked in. They had a seat on the couch facing the windows.

"Did you have any problems?" Constantin asked me.

"Nu (No)," I replied.

"Father is not exactly on board with my plan, but he isn't stepping in to stop it. In six months, I turn thirty and it will be time for me to take my rightful place."

"Are you ready?"

In order for my brother to take over as the Nasu he has to marry and produce an heir within a year of that marriage.

"Yes, Lizzy has been asking if we can move up the date of the wedding so that she can be pregnant by my birthday."

"It sounds like a solid plan."

"I'm not in a rush to stick my dick inside of my best friend."

Elizabeth Connor was Constantin's best friend. Her family lived next door to us and growing up, she used to follow behind us like a lost puppy. She had been in love with my brother forever but he did not see her in a romantic way. Nonetheless, we were not surprised when he announced who he would marry. Ever since then, she has been running around as if they were a couple and he let her because he knew what was required of him.

"It's not too late to find someone else."

"My plans are concrete. The next shipment is scheduled to be released in three weeks. Before that shipment, we need to figure out who is coming after us. I will come over this afternoon to see just how much Kofi knows how to do with a computer."

I believe if Constantin didn't have so many responsibilities already, he would have the time to crack the damn firewall protection himself.

"You know his schedule. Use your key to get in. I will tell him to expect you when I get home."

"There is no need. I will send him a text message."

Both Kenya and Kofi's cellphone numbers were in the background he collected on them. I already programmed them into my phone. I wonder what Kenya is doing right now.

"Is it strange living with five people?" Roman asked me.

"Strange, no. Different, yes. Kenya cooked us all breakfast this morning. They are taking the news well, almost too well."

"They are survivors, Alexandur. It has only been them two for years now and they have had to learn how to survive no matter what circumstances life threw at them," Roman replied.

"Why are you so vocal over them? We do not know them."

"You do not have to know people to know the type of person they are. Kofi is smarter than we realize. He will be a great asset to the family, and Kenya is a femme fatale. She is smart, beautiful, and dangerous."

"You are the second person today who has mentioned her looks. I would advise you to look elsewhere."

Roman smirked slightly before his face turned back to his stone impression. I shook my head.

"Brother, please do not fuck her. She is business," Constantine fussed.

"I know how to handle myself accordingly," I replied. They only stayed a couple more minutes before exiting my office. As soon as they walked out, I picked up my iPhone from the desk.

Kenya

Today was inventory day so I spent most of the day counting and checking supplies. Hooters opened at eleven and it has been pretty steady. Daytime was easier to manage than night. Nighttime was when the restaurant filled up with horny men ready to eat, drink, and flirt. A little after one, everything was running smoothly enough for me to sneak away to eat the salad I had one of the cooks make for me. The salad was topped with strawberries and almonds, and I couldn't wait to eat it. As soon as I took my first bite my iPhone dinged.

Unknown Number: I didn't like you laughing with my bodyguards this morning.

What the fuck. I been trying to get that crazy ass man off my mind all day and here he goes texting me.

Me: Would you rather I walk around with a frown on my face all day?

Unknown number: I just told you what I preferred. I do not like you flirting with them.

Me: Psycho man, I was not flirting with anybody. It is called being nice and having manners. You should really try it sometime.

Unknown number: Did Tree flirt with you on your way to work today?

Why does it matter and why am I smiling?

Unknown number: No. He was quiet the whole time now that I think about it. Did you say something to him? I do not know what about me gave the impression that I was a hoe, but I know how to be nice to men without spreading my legs wide open for them. What I do not understand is if I did fuck him, why should you care? You know I can fuck whoever I want, right?

My right leg had started to shake gently under my desk. Alexandur was out of his damn mind if he thought he could tell me what to do and what not to do. I saved his number under "TheDevil" then looked down at my salad and frowned. He had me so mad I no longer felt like eating. Ugh.

TheDevil: I do not make assumptions. I know you are not a whore. We have had a background check done on you and Kofi. Please refrain from ever mentioning you fucking again in my presence. I do not like it.

Me: That seems like a you problem. It is obvious you do not like a lot of things. Why are you messaging me bothering me Alexandur? Your bodyguards are handsome, but I am not thinking about either one of them. Now leave me alone.

TheDevil: I am messaging you because it will be safer for everyone involved if you knew what I like and what I did not like.

Is he threatening me or the lives of his bodyguards? Why was he so comfortable sending incriminating text messages? Ohhhhhhh, they probably got cops that work for them. Whew, my brain feels like it is about to explode.

I read the message over and over before deciding to lock my phone screen without responding. My life was crazy enough as it is without trying to decode the words of Alexandur Bucur.

God, I don't know which one of your angels lied to you and told you I was one of your toughest soldiers, but fire they ass immediately. Alexandur Bucur has only been in my life for two days and I do not see how you expect us not to kill each other.

The rest of my workday was spent trying to limit my interaction with people as much as possible. After the messages I received earlier, my attitude was not the best and I did not want to take it out on my staff or the customers. It was a little after eleven at night when me and Chris walked out of Hooters. I turned my back to lock the front doors. When I turned back around, I screamed.

"You scared the hell out of me. Why are you standing behind Chris like that?" I asked Tree. Tree just appeared out of nowhere. Chris frowned before turning around and almost bumping into him because he was standing so close to him.

"Why did he stay behind after everyone else left?"

Tree was talking about Chris as if they were not standing close enough to kiss each other.

"His name is Chris. He always stays behind at night to make sure I am safe. It can be dangerous at this time of the night; my car has been broken into twice," I replied in a calm voice. I was exhausted and trying hard not to let my temper out.

"Boss is not going to like that one bit. You are more than safe now; you do not need him to wait for you any longer."

Before I could cuss his ass out, Chris reached out to try to push him back. Crack. Tree grabbed his wrist and twisted it so fast I do not even know which way he turned it. Chris screamed out in pain and used his other hand to hold his wrist. I have never been so mad and embarrassed in my whole life. Without saying another word, I stomped across the street praying a car would hit me and take me out of my misery. Of course, my unlucky ass made it to Tree's black Ford F-150 truck unharmed. I snatched the passenger door and it opened. Grateful he had left it unlocked, I hopped inside his car and slammed the door. Tree opened the driver's side door and got in.

"I apologize if I have upset you, but if boss man finds out I let him walk you to my truck he will kill me and him. Alexandur texted me earlier and told me he did not want any males flirting with you," Tree said apologetically. I turned my head to look out the car window and bit down hard on my lip to keep myself from calling him and his boss everything but a child of God. The ride to Alexandur's house was full of tension. As soon as we made it there, I opened the door and jumped out. My feet were moving so fast I was surprised I didn't fall when I went up the stairs. Alexandur's room door was closed but I be damn if I respected his privacy when he was running around here issuing orders like a madman.

"Let me tell you something. I am a grown-ass woman. The last time I checked, my father was dead as a doorknob. You do not get the right to try to dictate who and what the hell I can do," I yelled loudly at Alexandur. Alexandur was scrolling on his phone lying on his pillow in his bed. He put the phone to the side and sat up to sit on the side of his bed. Before he could speak, my brother called my name.

"Kenya, you know you have to calm down. Stress is not good," he reminded me.

"It is okay, Kofi. I am sure whatever it is that has your sister so upset can be handled in a calm manner. If you could close the door to give the two of us a second to talk, I promise I will not hurt her. She will be in there to check on you shortly," Alexandur told Kofi. I chuckled sarcastically because there wasn't anything that I wanted to say to him that would be considered calm. Kofi looked at me and I nodded my head in confirmation. He looked at both of us before shaking his head and closing Alexandur's bedroom door.

"You spend too many hours at work. Why did you even go when you know you will be a millionaire in a few weeks?" he questioned me.

Inhale. Exhale. Inhale. Exhale. I closed my eyes and practiced some breathing techniques, praying that it stopped me from punching this man dead in his face. After a full minute of breathing deeply, I opened my eyes and looked at him.

"Alexandur, do you know Tree broke Chris's wrist tonight all because Chris waited for me? Chris has been waiting on me every night for over a year to make sure I am safe, and your bodyguard did some kind of weird ass karate move and hurt him all because of what you told him."

"I am failing to see the problem. Tree did what was expected of him. If you are looking for somebody to be mad at, be mad at yourself. You should have sent that little boy home when the rest of the crew left."

"Motherfucker, you don't get to tell me what the hell to do and you damn sure don't get to tell me who the hell I can talk to."

"Why do you feel like that?"

The calmness in his voice was making me even madder. He was sitting there talking to me like I was the one missing screws in my head when it was him.

Calm down, Kenya. Do not get you and Kofi killed. Reply back to his ass in the same calm manner.

"Alexandur, I understand that my brother is working for your family and y'all took me for collateral. I even understand that until you fully trust us you will have your bodyguard watching us. What I do not understand is the obsession you have with me and other men. I am a single woman who can do what I want."

"You are single, but you can't do what you want."

"Why. The. Hell. Not?"

I spoke slowly and pronounced each word clearly because I wanted to know what kind of twisted logic was swirling around up there in that empty ass head of his.

"From the moment I met you, you have bewitched me. I cannot seem to get you off my mind. Under normal circumstances, I would have fucked you and sent you on your way, but our circumstances are anything but normal. Mixing business with pleasure is a bad idea and something tells me I will not be satisfied with just one taste of you."

Silently, I stared at him while letting the words he just said process in my mind. *Did he just say he wanted to fuck me?*

"Yeah, that is a terrible idea. You kill people for a living and I work as a manager at Hooters. We are not compatible."

Instead of responding, he stood up. I was so upset when I

walked into the room, I did not even notice that he only had on a silk pair of pajama bottoms. Slowly, my eyes drifted from his eyes down to his naked chest and back up to his eyes. His cologne reached me before he did. It was not fair for him to look and smell so good.

"What kind of cologne is that?" I asked as he approached me. Instead of stopping in front of me, he slowly walked in a circle around me.

"It is a special blend of Baccarat. Francis Kurkdijan is a friend of the family. A couple of years ago he showed up to an event with a special blend he created exclusively for me and my brothers. We loved it. Now every few months we pay him a ridiculously large sum of money to have the personalized cologne shipped to us."

"The Devil wears Baccarat." I tried to joke to ease some of the tension floating around us.

Alexandur stopped walking and leaned in from behind me to sniff my neck. My heartbeat started racing fast, but I was not sure if it was from fear or lust.

"Do I scare you, Kenya?" he asked after he finished smelling my neck.

"Yes," I stuttered out.

"Smart girl, you should be scared. They call me the monstrul, that means monster in my native language. I am not the kind of man your parents warned you about. I'm the kind that they wouldn't dare speak of out of fear that I would appear."

In my mind, I knew I should have run out of his room, but my feet were stuck. His eyes had turned crazy and somehow he had inched even closer to me. Alexandur reached out and grabbed me by my neck tightly. It became hard to breathe, but I did not try to fight to get loose. Again, he leaned in and sniffed my neck while choking me. Gurgling noises were fighting to escape out of my mouth.

"I have never desired a woman like I desire you Kenya, and when I get you, I will destroy anything that gets in our way to keep you," he whispered in my ear. My vision blurred and tears fell from my eyes. I could feel my body getting weaker. He licked the left side of my face where my tears had fallen and then let me go. Without taking a moment to catch my breath, I ran out of his room. In the hallway, I fell against the wall and slumped to the floor. Air rushed inside of my lungs, and I took slow, steady breaths to calm my racing heart. Minutes passed by before I felt like I had the strength to get up and go to my room. When I stood, I lifted my head up and there he stood watching me. Without a second glance, I forced myself to walk serenely to my room and close the door.

Alexandur

I lay in bed replaying everything that had just happened. Kenya was my gift from heaven or hell. Either way, I felt a feeling inside of me that I had never felt before about any other woman. It was not until I wrapped my hands around her neck that I accepted what I had been fighting the last couple of days. She was made for me, and I was made for her. Never had I seen anything more beautiful than when she cried for me. Her eyes were begging me to squeeze her neck tighter. She forced herself to remain still even after feeling herself getting dangerously close to passing out. It had to have been at the minimum thirty minutes since she fled out of my bedroom, and I could still smell her scent every time I inhaled. My dick jumped in my briefs, begging for some kind of release. My hand went under the cover to free my dick.

I closed my eyes and imagined Kenya standing in front of me naked. Her chocolate skin glowing in the darkness. Her brown nipples hard and begging for my attention.

"Get on your knees Kenya, like a good slut." *She licked her juicy ass lips, taunting me, before falling to her knees to do as I said.*

"Open your mouth and show me your tongue." *She opened her mouth wide and stuck her tongue out.*

"Fuck," I groaned, before spitting on both of my hands and grabbing my dick hard. Slowly, I stroked my dick up and down while imagining me slapping both sides of her cheeks.

"Don't stop sucking my dick until I come down your throat," I grunted out, before opening my mouth to spit a big glob onto her tongue. I watched my spit drip slowly down her jaw and onto her neck before I grabbed a hand full of her hair and thrust my dick into her mouth. "Fuck, Kenya," I moaned her name out while fucking her face roughly. She knows how much I like to see her cry for me. She looked at me with her eyes full of tears and moaned, creating a tingling sensation around my dick.

I stroked my dick harder, feeling my nut quickly approaching.

Kenya took her index finger on her left hand and wet it with some of our spit that had fallen. She then took that same finger and slid it inside of my ass.

"Fuck!" I screamed and then held her head tight so that she had no choice but to swallow every drop of nut I had just released into her mouth.

Slowly, I opened my eyes and looked at the mess I created on my hands. My dick spurted out so much nut that it was all over my briefs. I tossed the covers back and got out of my bed to wash up. By the time I changed and climbed back into my bed, I went straight to sleep.

The next morning, I woke up feeling like the king of the world. During my gym routine, I thought about Kenya and what I should do next. I had to approach our situation like I did everything else in my life. The only thing that mattered was winning. In order for me to win, every step had to be calculated and executed perfectly. It is like looking at a chess board and deciding which moves to make so that I can conquer my opponent's king. Ironically, just like the Queen piece in chess, Kenya was the one with the power, but I could not let her realize that yet. Last night had to have scared and confused her. If I move too fast, I will reveal my plans too soon. She knows that I have a deep desire for her, but she has no idea that I meant what I said about keeping her. For the rest of her life, she will belong to me and me only. In Robert Greene's book, *The Art of Seduction*, it stressed the importance of not showing how interested you are, especially in the beginning. After last night's admission, I now had to force myself to pull back. Today I will have a bouquet of black roses delivered to her job. During ancient Greece and Roman times black roses were associated with power and death. I needed her to understand the bond she was weaving around me was a powerful and deadly bond. The note will read *to my light from your dark* and nothing else. After I send the roses, I will only speak to her if she speaks to me first. I will make myself scarce, only appearing when necessary but always watching her from a distance. The next few days are going to be hard as hell for me, but the prize will be worth it in the end. It is not every day a monster like me is blessed to find a woman who has the capabilities to be his perfect counterpart. Kenya Jones will be my wife, and she will be my wife very fucking soon.

Kenya

"What happened last night?" Kofi asked me. I should have been surprised that he showed up in the kitchen a little earlier than normal, but I was not. After I made it back to my room safely last night, I did not go back out to check on him.

"Your new boss man is determined to drive me crazy, but it's not anything I can't handle."

"He likes you Kenya, and that worries me."

"He does not like me; he is just bored and wants to fuck me. You need to remain focused on finding out the information they want so they do not kill us."

"Constatin was right about the owner of the laptop being intelligent. Every time I think I am close to creaking the firewall protection, I hit a dead space."

"You are the smartest person in the whole world, so I have no doubt you will figure it out."

Kofi laughed and the sound put a smile on my face. I walked over to the refrigerator to pull some food items out. Alexandur's refrigerator was fully stocked but I needed to ask him if Tree could take me to the grocery store to get a few more items.

"You are just saying that because I am your brother."

"Perhaps. I love you, Kofi. I feel like I have not done a good enough job being there for you and protecting you, but I will give my last breath to make sure you are okay."

"I love you even more, Kenya. You are more than just my sister; you are my best friend. You were forced to raise me by yourself and look how smart I am."

I laughed and shook my head.

"Boy please, your Jimmy Neutron head ass came out smart."

"Facts. If they let me, I want to continue working for the Mafia. It is more money and exciting," Kofi admitted.

My eyes closed for a quick second before opening them back up and then turning around to look at my brother.

"Kofi, this is not something to play with. I understand you are basically being forced to work with them anyway, but only as their tech guy. Please do not try to get more involved with the Mafia. I do not want to lose you."

"I won't, Kenya," he replied. I turned back and around and continued cooking breakfast. Silently, I prayed that God protected my brother because I knew he was lying. If given the opportunity, he would involve himself even deeper with the Mafia. I could not let that happen.

"What up," Kofi said before I heard chairs being moved around. It was too early for Alexandur to be in the kitchen. For the last couple of days, he always worked out first, showered, and got dressed, and then came down to eat breakfast. Breakfast only took about fifteen minutes to make. As I fixed the plates, I heard footsteps approaching me.

"Good morning, ma'am, I can carry the plates to the table for you," Tree said shyly.

"Good morning, and thanks, I appreciate it," I replied. I smiled at him to let him know I forgave him for acting an ass last night. He was only doing his job.

"Why are you so close to her?" Alexandur asked, startling both of us. Tree rushed to pick the plates up and take them to the table without responding. I looked up to give his mean ass the evil eye, but he had already sat down at the table and started talking to my brother. After delivering the last few plates to the table, I sat down to eat. Everybody ate and had casual conversation. Every few minutes I would look up at Alexandur, but his attention was elsewhere. He finished eating first and left shortly after. We did not exchange any words with each other. Something was off but I could not figure out what it was.

Maybe he changed his mind about desiring me after I left his room last night? Good.

I did not feel so good about it though. If anything, it made me wonder what was going through his mind. Kofi and Hero were the next ones out the door. Tree and I left five minutes later after I cleaned the kitchen up. On the way to Hooters, I replayed everything that happened between Alexandur and me last night. He clearly wanted me last night. How could that change so fast and why? By the time I walked into work, I made up my mind that I was not going to think about the crazy ass, confusing man all day. If he did not find me attractive anymore then it was his loss. My iPhone dinged and I hurried into my office to pull my phone out to see who it was.

Chris: I cannot come to work today. My wrist is broken, thanks for asking, but I will be able to come back in a week.

Fuck, I am being a terrible boss and friend. I should have checked on Chris last night.

Me: I am so sorry. It is not that I do not care, I just wanted to get away from here so that Tree would leave. Last night was my fault. My new friends are not exactly nice people. Please accept my apology. I will update the schedule shortly. I am glad you are okay, and I will see you in a week.

Chris: Friend? Shit, the way ol' boy was acting it seems like his boss is more than just your friend. You told me you were not interested in dating. Shit crazy!

Was I wrong for not checking on Chris? Yes, I was very wrong, he had been a good friend to me. Did I owe him any explanation about my dating life? No, I have told him repeatedly that I was not interested in him romantically. I thumbs upped the message without responding. I only had a couple of hours to replace all five of his shifts and update the schedule for all the employees to see it. After everything was fixed, I left my office and began getting the restaurant ready for when we opened. The rest of the day went by smoothly. Alexandur kept popping up in my mind, but I tried my best to clear the thoughts as soon as they appeared.

"Kenya, you have a delivery here that you have to sign for," one of my waitresses came into the kitchen to tell me.

"Be right back," I told the chef and walked out to see what it was. When I made it to the front of the restaurant the waitress that came and got me was standing next to a man with a bouquet of flowers in one hand and a clipboard in the other. Frowning, I approached them.

"Who are you looking for?" I asked the delivery guy.

"Kenya Jones. Is that you ma'am?"

Instead of responding, I nodded my head.

"Sign here."

He pushed the clipboard and a pen into my hand. Quickly, I scribbled my signature on the first line I saw. He handed the bouquet of roses to me and waved goodbye. Confused, I looked at the black roses before smelling them. They smelled divine. I walked over to the bar to place the bouquet down and grab the note. The note was short and sweet, so it didn't take long to read. After reading the note, I was even more confused. Alexandur had sent me roses, did that mean he did still like me? I carried the roses to my office to put them on my desk while I worked. For the rest of my shift, I would sneak into my office to smell my roses. On the note that came with the flowers, he said I was the light and he was the dark. How did a person of the light get tangled up with a person of the dark without mixing colors? I did not think that was possible, but what did I know? After work, Tree was standing at the door waiting on me. This time he made sure I did not cross the street without looking both ways as if I were a child. I wonder if I were to get romantically involved with Alexandur would that mean I would have a permanent bodyguard always watching my every move.

Yeah, no, that's not happening. Why was I even thinking about dating a man like him anyway?

I tried to clear my thoughts of him and tune into the country music Tree was listening to in the background, but it did not work.

Okay, I like him. Out of the men who have tried to talk to me the last couple of years, he is the only one who I cannot get off my mind. I did not even think about Keith this much and I was in a relationship with him for years.

When we made it to Alexandur's house I hoped that he would be up and out of his room, but when I made it up the stairs his door was closed. I walked up to his bedroom door and placed my right ear against it to see if I could hear him, but it was silent. Disappointed, I went to my room and took my shower. After I got dressed for bed, I left back out of my room to check on Kofi. He was in his bed sleep. On the way back to my room, I was tempted to creep over to Alexandur's bedroom door again, but I did not. Exhaustion finally hit when I crawled into the bed and under the covers.

The next four days were the same. Alexandur had not said anything at all to me. If we were in the same room, he would look everywhere but at me. I do not know what kind of games he was playing, but he could play them by himself.

Alexandur

I sat quietly in the corner and watched as Kenya's body rose up and down. Every night she slept in the same position on her stomach. She was a hard sleeper and did not toss or turn. On her body were always some shorts and either a big t-shirt or a tank top. When I checked her dressers, she had a whole dresser drawer full of sexy lingerie and night clothes to wear, but she preferred to sleep more comfortably. On her head was the same big hair cloth thing.

I watched her silently for an hour or so more before standing up and walking over to the bed. I leaned down and rubbed my nose into her neck before placing a soft kiss there. This morning at breakfast, she looked at me with anger in her eyes. I acted like I did not notice it, but I noticed everything about her. Quietly, I turned away from her bed and walked silently out of her bedroom.

The next morning, I woke up with a smile. Kenya had had enough time to herself. Kofi was spending the weekend with Constatin. He was close to breaking into the laptop and Constatin wanted to see if he could help him. Me and Kenya would have the whole west wing to ourselves. I jumped out of my bed and made it up, before going to my bathroom to handle my hygiene. Afterward, I went to the gym to do my workout. An hour later I was walking into the kitchen.

"Good morning, everyone."

Everybody got quiet and looked at me like I had two horns sticking out of my head. Instead of asking them what in the hell were they looking at, I took my normal seat at the head of the table. A couple of minutes later, Kenya walked over and placed a plate of food in front of me. I don't know if somebody taught Kenya how to cook or if she taught herself, but the damn woman made the healthiest of meals taste delicious.

"You ready, Tree?" Kenya asked.

"Yes ma'am," he replied and stood up to take his plate to the sink.

"Why are you leaving so early? You normally are the last two to leave," I asked her.

"I'm surprised you even paid that much attention to know that," her smart ass replied before walking out of the kitchen.

Damn, she was pissed. I cannot wait to fuck that attitude right up out of her.

Kenya never returned to the kitchen. In fact, I heard the front door slam a couple minutes after she walked out of here. Kofi laughed and shook his head.

"What's wrong with her?" I asked him, even though I already knew the answer.

"She had been nice to all of us, you just get on her nerves."

This time Hero and I laughed.

"Well, little brother, the feeling is mutual. Your sister drives me crazy too."

"I know you like her, but she has been through a lot. If you plan to play with her heart, leave her alone now."

Look at him trying to protect his sister.

"Kenya is going to be my wife and nothing or no one is going to stop that."

He was quiet for a few moments before he nodded his head.

"I'm cool with it, good luck getting her to say I do though."

This time we both laughed together. He and Hero stayed a few more minutes before getting up to leave. Kenya only had to work today; she was off tomorrow. When she became my wife, she was not working so many hours. It was too dangerous, and I did not like her being away from me for so long.

When I made it to work, I did not stay in my office for long before it was time to head downstairs for testing. Testing did not end until after lunch, but I did not have a big appetite anyway. Instead, I sat at my desk and thought about Kenya. After a few seconds, I decided to text her a message.

Me: How is your day going sotie (wife)?

I held my iPhone in my hand for a few minutes waiting for a response. When I did not get one, I put my iPhone back on my desk and turned toward my computer to work. Some of the security guards had lost some of their equipment and I needed to order some more hats. I logged on to my computer and got busy. Ten minutes later I finally heard my iPhone ding.

This is why she can't work as much when we get married. Look how long it took her to respond.

Unfortunately, when I unlocked my iPhone, the message was not from her.

Mama: Why haven't I seen you in over a week fiul (son)?
Me: I apologize Mama, I will stop by to see you after work.
Mama: Thank you.

Kenya really is upset over me giving her the cold shoulder for a few days.

Instead of sitting my iPhone back down, I decided to send Kenya another message.

Me: I do not like it when you don't answer me in a timely manner!

This time after I sent the text message, I closed my phone screen and put it back down on my desk. For the next couple of hours, I concentrated only on work and not on wrapping my fingers around Kenya's neck and choking the shit out of her for being so stubborn. After I finished working, I headed over to visit my mom.

"Mama," I yelled out when I entered my parents' house. A minute later, I heard my mama's soft footsteps coming down the stairs.

"Fiul (son)," she said. I waited until she was close to me to reach down to give her a hug and a kiss.

"Are you hungry?"

"Actually, I missed lunch today Mama, so I am."

"Come on into the kitchen so I can make you and the bodyguards something quick to eat for dinner."

"Da Mama (Yes Mama)," I replied and followed her into the kitchen. Tom's car was not parked out front when I pulled up so he and my father must be out handling business. As soon as I entered Mama's kitchen my mind went to my stubborn sotie (wife).

"Mama, will you make plenty of food?"

"Da (Yes), is it for the woman staying with you? Constatin says you have a crush."

Constatin talked to fucking much!

"Da Mama (Yes Mama), she will be my future sotie (wife)."

Mama stopped pulling food out of the refrigerator to turn and look at me. I held my head high and let her look into my eyes to let her see how serious I was.

"Can she handle your monster?" Mama asked me softly.

"I believe so, Mama. She is very stubborn, but I cannot get her off my mind."

Mama smiled before coming over to kiss me on my cheek.

"She is the one when she can handle your monster. Do not hide who you are from her. If she can handle all parts of you, bring her to meet me."

"Da Mama (Yes Mama)," I replied.

While Mama cooked, she asked me random questions and I answered each one of them honestly. I did not keep secrets from my mama and hopefully, me and Kenya will be able to be the same way one day. Dinner only took an hour to cook. She made us a big pot of smoky bean stew. Once the pot had cooled down enough for me to leave with it, I kissed my mother goodbye and left. By the time I made it home, it was going on ten at night. Kenya always comes home around eleven thirty. While I waited for her to get here, I took my shower and put on my night clothes. Time was moving quickly and before I knew it my iPhone was saying it was eleven forty-five. Concerned, I unlocked my phone and called Tree.

"Where the hell are y'all?"

"Sorry boss. Kenya did not come out of work until eleven thirty."

"Why? Was something wrong?"

Tree got silent before I heard him take a deep breath.

"No, nothing was wrong. She decided to have a couple of shots with her friend before leaving work.

"Friend? Kenya does not have any friends that work with her. Do not fucking play with me! Give me a name."

"Chris."

As soon as I heard the name, I hung up my iPhone.

Kenya

My day had been nothing but hell. Two waitresses called in at the last minute leaving us short staffed. We were managing things at first until an hour before the football game came on. The restaurant got packed and it seemed like everybody that came was already drunk when they walked through the door. It had been months since I took over a waitressing shift and after tonight, I hope it will be months again. The only positive thing I can say about today was that in under six hours, I made almost five hundred dollars in tips. I gathered my stuff together and locked my office up. When I made it to the front Chris was still standing behind the bar. Today was his first day back and we had not said more than a few words to each other, but I didn't take it personal. We had been too busy at work to even think about carrying on a casual conversation.

"Why are you still here, and what are you doing?"

"It was stupid of me to return to work on a Friday. My hand is killing me and the pain medicine I took before I came to work wore off hours ago."

My eyes went to the cast on his wrist, and I felt terrible inside. Instead of fussing at him about drinking the company's alcohol without paying for it, I walked over to the bar and had a seat.

"You want a shot?" he asked me.

I was not a heavy drinker, but I figured a couple of shots would not have a huge effect on me. Plus, I was not in a rush to get back to Alexandur's house. Alexandur had decided to message me today all cordial and shit as if he had not ignored me for days. On top of that, he called me sotie and I could not believe my eyes when I googled the translation of the word. That crazy ass man had the audacity to call me his wife after treating me like Casper's ghost ass.

Chris fixed me a shot of D'usse and then himself another one. He picked the shot glass up and drank it fast. I copied his actions and did exactly what he did. I damn near died. My throat was on fire, and I almost threw up trying to swallow that nasty ass shit down. Chris was laughing at me so hard he was choking.

"Yo, why you swallow it like that? You do not sip a shot down. You have to throw the shot straight to the back of your throat and swallow it fast," he informed me when he calmed down enough from laughing to get the words out.

"That shit nasty, and it burns," I replied.

"It is not supposed to taste good; its only job is to get you drunk. Here, try it one more time."

Chris made me another shot and I stared at it for a few seconds before throwing caution to the wind and trying it again. It was worse the second time. Before I could tell him that though, there was a hard knock at the door.

"There go your peoples. Tell him I do not want any trouble tonight. Matter fact, you leave out first so he will not attack me again," Chris said before shaking his head.

Oh fuck, I forgot all about Tree being outside waiting on me.

"I will not let him attack you, but we really do have to go. Tonight was a one-time thing; you know I do not allow you guys to drink for free."

Chris nodded his head in agreement, but his eyes were on the door of the restaurant. He put the bottle of D'usse back on the alcohol shelf and walked from around the bar to where I stood.

"When we make it out the door just go ahead to your car and let me handle my friend," I warned him. Chris looked at me like no shit Sherlock, and together we walked to the door. One of the waitresses had locked the door as soon as the last customer left and I kept it locked until it was time for me to go. I twisted the lock to disengage it and pushed the door open. Tree glared at Chris as soon as we walked out of the restaurant together. Chris dropped his head and rushed off toward where his car was parked.

"Drive safe," I yelled out after him. He did not even turn around to give me a response. I wondered how many shots he had in all, while I watched him crank his car up and pull out of the parking lot. He was not driving erratically, but I planned on fussing at him the next time I saw him about drinking and driving. Suddenly, my body got hot, and I felt a little woozy.

"Come on Ms. Kenya, not only are you late, but you have been drinking."

His tone was not nice, and I was not in the mood for a pointless argument. I did not have to answer to him or his crazy ass boss. We crossed the street and got inside his truck. Before he could pull off, his iPhone rang. Tree cursed before answering the phone. The call did not have to be on speakerphone for me to figure out it was Alexandur calling and asking questions about me.

"He could have just called my phone," I mumbled to Tree when he hung up the phone. Tree did not respond, but he did look at me with worry in his eyes. At that point, I was tired, aggravated, and tipsy. I laid my head back against the seat and closed my eyes.

"Wake up, Ms. Kenya, we are here," Tree said gently. He was shaking my shoulder while he talked. I opened my eyes and looked around. We were in front of Alexandur's house; I had slept the whole ride. Tree got out of his truck and walked around to open the door for me. Neither one of us said anything else to each other as he put in the house alarm code. When the door unlocked, Tree went his way, and I went mine. It was quiet as I walked up the stairs. When I made it to the hallway, Alexandur's bedroom door was shut. He was the most confusing man I had ever met. What was the point in calling Tree to ask questions about me if he did not even plan to talk to me? Officially over the entire day, I hurried into my bedroom. Within twenty minutes, I had showered, got dressed, and climbed my ass into bed to go to sleep.

Music. Someone was playing music in my dream. It was a dramatic but beautiful sound. I enjoyed the music until I heard humming. Somebody was humming along to the music playing.

Open your eyes Kenya, NOW.

Slowly, I opened my eyes. The music continued playing. I had never heard the song before, but opera was not something I was familiar with. I turned around on my back and jumped.

"It's about time you woke up, we been waiting on you."

Alexandur stood over the bed looking down at me as he spoke.

What the fuck? Wait, did he say we?

I sat up in the bed and almost pissed myself. At the foot of the bed was Chris tied up to a chair. He had tape over his mouth and tears running down his face.

"Alexandur, what the fuck is wrong with you? Why is Chris here?" I asked him slowly. He did not respond, but he didn't have to because his eyes had turned crazy looking and I knew the monster inside of him was in control.

"Alexandur, please don't do anything crazy," I begged him. He smiled at me before walking to the foot of the bed where Chris was. My heart was beating so fast I could feel it hitting hard against my chest. Alexandur cocked back and punched Chris in his face twice, busting his lip. I jumped out of bed but before I could make it to them, Alexandur pulled his gun out and placed it to Chris's head. I froze and tears started to fall down my face.

"Does he mean so much to you that you dare go against me?"

Alexandur's voice was darker than I had ever heard it before.

"He is just my friend," I tried to plead with him.

"I do not believe you. I think you like him and he likes you. What is the problem with that, Kenya?"

The problem is you are a fucking psycho!

"I don't like him romantically; he is just my friend."

"Prove it."

"Huh?" I stuttered out.

How in the fuck can I prove I do not like him when you got him chained to a fucking chair?

"Take off all your clothes, Kenya."

It took a few seconds for the words that he had just said to process in my mind. Those seconds were too long for him though, because he took the gun and started bashing Chris in the face with it. Growing up, I had heard of people getting pistol whooped, but seeing it was horrible. The gun made a sound every time it connected to his face. Blood was leaking from various places on his face, and I could hear him groaning out in pain from behind the tape he had on his mouth.

"Please, please stop hitting him. Look, I am taking off all my clothes."

My voice was so weak and scary that it sounded foreign to my own ears. Quickly, I started removing everything I had on and tossing it on the floor. Within a minute I stood in front of them naked and shaking.

"Sit on the edge of the bed and don't fucking move."

Without responding, I quickly did what he asked of me. Alexandur slipped his gun back into his pants and walked toward me. I looked up at him pleadingly. His right hand reached out and grabbed me by my throat. He squeezed so tight that I instantly felt lightheaded. This was not like the first time when he choked me. This time I think he really was about to kill me. My hands went up to the hand he had around my throat. I tried my best to pull it from around my neck, but he would not budge. After about thirty seconds of fighting, my hands felt too heavy and I dropped them back to my sides.

"Good girl," he praised me before letting my neck go. I sucked in big gulps of air trying to fill my lungs back up as quickly as possible. Alexandur reached down and gently rubbed the backside of his fingers down my face.

"You are so fucking beautiful, Kenya. I love it when you cry."

He lifted my head to look at him before lowering his lips to join them with my lips. His kiss was soft, and I was not expecting that. He kissed me so deeply that it almost felt like he did so in a loving manner. My mouth opened slightly, and our tongues touched before dancing together erotically. The kiss went on and on until I was out of breath and my pussy was wet and aching for some attention.

"Open your fucking eyes and look at Chris. I want him to see that you belong to me and me only," Alexandur stopped kissing me and whispered into my ear. My eyes flew open, and it felt like someone had tossed a bucket of ice on my body.

Oh my god, what the fuck is wrong with me?

My eyes joined with Chris's and a sob escaped my mouth. For a moment, I forgot where I was and what was happening.

"Don't stop looking at him, I want him to see me make my pussy cum," Alexandur demanded. Chris's eyes were almost swollen shut, but I could see them open up a little more when he heard what Alexandur had just said. Alexandur dropped to his knees and spread my legs wide.

"No, no, noooooo," I cried out and then gasped. Alexandur sucked my whole clit into his mouth. I tried to push his head away, but he just sucked on my clit harder. I felt his finger touch my pussy before he slid two fingers inside of me. He fucked me hard with his fingers while sucking on my clit, occasionally letting his tongue flick up and down. My teeth went down hard on my bottom lip to fight the moans that were trying to come out of my mouth. My eyes closed and a sensation like I had never felt before flowed all over my body.

"Open your fucking eyes," Alexandur said. My eyes opened but I stared at the wall. I could not look Chris in his face while Alexandur used my body in such a fucking sick way.

"Good girl, my pussy is so responsive. She is so wet that the sheets are soaked," he said before putting his head back between my legs and licking my clit up and down. My hands clutched the cover on the bed, and I tried hard to stop myself from cumming but it just made my body shake even more.

"AHHHHHHHHHHHH," I screamed aloud. There were no words to explain the feeling of ecstasy that coursed through my body while I came repeatedly in his mouth. The pleasure felt so good that it became painful at the same time.

"Fuck, I can't wait to feel my pussy."

Alexandur stood and unbuttoned his pants. He pulled his dick out of his briefs and stroked it up and down fast. His dick was about eight inches long and thick as a water bottle.

"Keep your legs open like that and don't fucking move. I want to nut all over my pussy."

He stroked himself faster and then groaned. Hot spurts of nut shot out of his dick and onto my stomach and pussy. When he finished nutting, he stuck his dick back in his pants and buttoned them back up. I thought he was done but instead, he leaned down and rubbed his nut into my stomach and pussy as if it were body lotion. After he finished, he stuck one of his fingers in his mouth and sucked it. Speechless and exhausted, I watched as he walked back over to Chris.

"Alexandur, I did everything you asked. He knows I belong to you now, please let him go."

You could hear the defeat in my voice. I knew if I got up it would set him off even more.

"Why in the world would I let him live after flirting with my sotie and then watching her cum?" he asked me like I was dumb.

"You forced him to watch, you fucking psycho," I yelled at him. Tears were falling down my face again and I felt sick to my stomach. Alexandur bent down toward his feet and pulled his pant leg up. His leg had a knife strapped to it. He unstrapped the knife and stood up.

"Did you know Chris had a girlfriend and kids?" he asked me.

"No, you know I did not know. Look, you made your point. If you do this, I won't ever talk to you again."

"I guess we will have a silent marriage then," he replied before sticking his hand into Chris's left eye. He held his eyeball steady with one hand and used the other to cut in a circular motion around it. He stopped cutting and pulled his eyeball out. I started gagging.

"Sotie, baby, if you close your eyes again, I will spend all night killing him and I know you are tired. You may lay right there but do not close your eyes again. I want you to know what I am going to do to every man who looks at you with sexual desire."

Alexandur's sick ass did the same thing to right eye before putting them into Chris's mouth. He then took his knife and stabbed him repeatedly in the stomach. For the rest of my life, I will never be able to get the images of tonight out of my mind. By the time he stood up and licked his knife, I no longer felt like a human. It was like I was there physically, but mentally I had checked out.

"I am about to run you a warm bath. By the time you come out of the tub, the bodyguards will have this mess cleaned up. Tomorrow you will move into my room. This carpet will need to be removed and replaced."

"Go to hell," I whispered.

He chuckled before walking into the bathroom. I could hear the water running in the bathroom, but I did not get up. It was my fault Chris was dead. Alexandur told me he was a monster, he warned me to keep other men away from me. A man was just brutally murdered in front of my eyes and if I had just fucking listened, he would still be alive.

"Come on, my beautiful sotie," Alexandur said a few minutes later. He scooped me up bridal style in his arms and carried me to the bathroom. Gently, he lowered my body down into the bath water. He had made the temperature of the water hot. It was almost too hot, but my body relaxed slightly in appreciation.

"Do you need me to bathe you?" he asked me. I quickly shook

my head no. He leaned down and placed a kiss on my forehead before standing up and walking out of the bathroom. Exhausted, I closed my eyes and leaned my head against the back of the tub. I am not a weak person; I have gone through so much in life and survived it all. This time though, I do not know if I can make it through. Tears blurred my vision again. I had not cried this much since the last time my world was flipped upside down.

I have to get the hell away from here. If I can make it to Constatin or Roman, I can beg and plead for them to let me stay with them while my brother figures everything out.

My thoughts were running rapidly through my mind. If I got away from here, I could call my brother and ask for a meeting with Constatin. I doubt they will let me completely go but they might let me stay with one of them.

120429, 120429, 120429

I had watched Tree put the house alarm code in several times. Instead of going to sleep, I was going to pack a small bag of clothes and get out of here. My eyes opened back up and I stared straight ahead at the wall. Images of Chris's eyeless body floated into my mind, and I had to bite the back of my hand to stop from crying out loud.

God, please forgive me for what I have done.

I am not sure how long I stayed in the bathtub. The water had turned cold and the skin on my fingers was wrinkled when I finally forced myself to get up. After wrapping a big white towel around my body, I opened the bathroom door and peeked out. The room was empty and Chris's body was gone. On the carpet was a big red bloodstain, but other than that the room looked like nothing had happened. As I got closer to the bed, I noticed he had changed the sheets too. I walked to the closet and put on a pair of black leggings and a t-shirt. On the closet floor was my black over-the-shoulder bag. I did not even look at what clothes I grabbed, I just stuffed as many clothes as I could inside my bag and walked out of the closet. Before climbing into the bed, I put my black bag beside the bed and grabbed my iPhone. The time read one seventeen in the morning. Alexandur got up every morning at five, so I set the alarm on my phone for four in the morning. I turned the volume down so that only I would hear it when it went off. Finally, I closed my eyes and let the darkness take me over.

Beep. Beep. Beep. The alarm on my phone went off right beside the left side of my face. I groaned and opened my eyes. Flashbacks of what had happened a few hours earlier played in my mind, and I jumped out of my bed. My black bag was still beside the bed packed and ready to go. I slipped on my house shoes, grabbed the bag, unplugged my phone charger, and walked to the bedroom door.

He is going to kill me.

Fear made me pause before reaching down to grab the bedroom doorknob and turning it. The doorknob did not turn. Frantically, I tried twisting and twisting it before I realized I had been locked inside of the room from the outside.

"ALEXANDUR, ALEXANDUR!" I yelled out loudly before beating on the door with my hands.

Fuck, fuck, fuck!

My iPhone rang and I saw thedevil pop up on the screen.

"Let me out of here!" I yelled into the phone as soon as I connected the call.

"No. You need time to calm down. You are not thinking rationally."

"Rationally? Alexandur, let me the fuck out of this room."

"I already told you I was not. Get back in bed and go back to sleep. In the morning, we will talk when you have calmed down more."

"Open the door or I will call the police."

"Go right ahead. The police are only going to call me and tell me everything you said. If you would like to try your luck though, sotie, you have my permission. I will not like it though, and you know how things turn out when I do not like something."

"You sick bastard, I don't care if you kill me. At this point, death will be better anyway."

"Do not be silly. I told you you're not thinking rationally. I will never hurt you, sotie. Well, not in the way you are speaking of. Now I cannot say the same about your best friend in Alabama. I do not like upsetting you, but you have been an unbelievably bad girl tonight."

My heart stopped. Of course, he would know about Ari. Without thinking, I threw my phone against the wall and listened to it shatter.

Alexandur

Frustrated, I ran hard on the treadmill. Kenya was the only person on this earth who could make me react off emotion. I wanted to have more time to show her that I was the man for her, but she just had to be hardheaded. The taste of her pussy was addictive and if we were not having a minor disagreement, my face would be back in between her legs. I hit the stop button on the treadmill and got off it. Sweat had my gym clothes clinging tightly to my body. Angrily, I wiped my face with my hand before striding to the shower. After my shower, my mood was a little better but not by much. Before I approached Kenya with breakfast, I had to get my emotions in check. When I walked into the kitchen, Tree and Hero sat at the table eating some of the stew my mother made. Without saying a word to either one of them, I walked over to the refrigerator. Kenya has mentioned on more than one occasion that she liked to eat healthy, but I wanted her to try a traditional Romanian breakfast. For lunch I will warm her some stew. I gathered the few items I needed to make her gris cu lapte (semolina with milk). Gris cu lapte is my and my brothers' favorite breakfast meal. Our mama would make it at least once a week for us when we were younger. When I finished making it, I decided to cut up some raspberries and strawberries to eat with her meal. I arranged everything together on a tray and carried it up upstairs. At her bedroom door, I had to hold the tray carefully with one hand so that I could take the keys out of my pocket and unlock the door.

"Good morning, beautiful," I said to her when I entered the bedroom. Kenya was lying in the bed curled up on her side staring at the wall.

"I cooked you breakfast."

Silence. I walked over to the nightstand by the bed and sat the tray of food on top of it.

"Kenya, I know you are upset and that is okay. I will leave you alone to think some more after you eat. I made you my favorite Romanian breakfast."

Her stubborn ass still did not respond to me.

"Do we have to do this the hard way? I just want to feed you, sotie."

Kenya remained silent. I walked over to the bed and tried to reach out to touch her, but she turned her face away from me. It was taking everything in me not to remind her that she was mine and I could touch her whenever I wanted.

"You have a choice, you can let me watch you eat breakfast, or I can call the bodyguard in here to hold you down while I feed you."

That pissed her off because she pushed the cover off her body and sat up on the edge of the bed. She still avoided my gaze and remained silent, but she reached out to pick up the tray of food. She sat the tray of food on her lap and ate like she was starved. In three minutes, she had eaten all the gris cu lapte and fruit. The only thing she did not touch was the orange juice.

"Do you not like orange juice? I can go fix you something else to drink."

Kenya stood up and placed the food tray back down on the nightstand. She climbed back into the bed and pulled the cover all the way over her whole body including her face. I chuckled and shook my head.

"My mama cooked a stew for us to eat last night, but you were too busy getting drunk with a dead man. When I come back with your lunch Kenya, we will talk. I have never been in a relationship before, but I know not communicating with each other is bad for our relationship."

I stood up and picked up the empty food tray. After closing her bedroom door, I locked it again and walked back down the stairs to the kitchen.

Kenya

It had been a few hours since Alexandur left. I only got up once to check to see if the door was locked. When I confirmed it was, I climbed back into the bed. Stress had some of the joints in my hands and feet swelling up. Tonight, I would have to soak in an Epsom salt bath to help the swelling go down. My thoughts wandered back to Alexandur and the situation we were in. I do not understand what was so special about me that he was determined to have me. He claims that he has never felt this way before about another woman, but I don't know if I believe him. Knock, knock, knock. Speak of the devil and he shall appear. Alexandur knocked on the door three times before I heard keys jiggling and then the door open. He strolled into the room still dressed in the same clothes he had on this morning. This was my first time seeing him in sweatpants and a tank top. The man was evil as fuck but there was no denying he was disgustingly handsome.

"Baby, I know I said we would talk when I brought your stew, but we might as well go ahead and talk while the stew is warming up on the stove."

I took a couple of deep breaths before sitting up in the bed to look at him.

"Your anger is misplaced. Not only did I warn you, but Tree told Chris to no longer wait for you. Every action has a reaction."

"You are insane. It is not okay for you to kill people just because they do something you do not like. Hell, I don't like paying my taxes, but I can't go kill everybody at the IRS building, now can I?"

"I would not advise it. The IRS has thousands of employees in one building. Unless you had access to nuclear weapons like I do then you are only going to get yourself killed."

That's. Not. The. Point.

"You are missing the point on purpose. What's the point of having this conversation if you don't think you did anything wrong?"

"The point is for us to communicate openly and honestly so that we can move past this. I do not feel wrong about killing Chris. If anything, I should have killed his whole fucking family."

My mouth dropped open and I stared at him. At this point, nothing he said should shock me, but my God, this man was so cold.

"Why me, Alexandur? If you want to go around murdering everybody who pisses you off that's your karma, but why do I have to be involved in it?"

Alexandur walked over to the edge of the bed and had a seat. He was close enough to me that he could reach out and touch me if he wanted to, but also far away enough that he was not invading my personal space.

"That is not a question I know the answer to. You feel the same pull to me that I feel to you, you just feel like it is wrong, so you fight it. Ask whichever higher power you believe in, but I do not know."

"That is because it is wrong, Alexandur. I was not raised in a ruthless ass Mafia family. I have feelings and emotions like a normal human being. People are dying for no reason, and I am not okay with that."

"Let me ask you a couple of simple questions, and I want you to answer them truthfully, Kenya."

I rolled my eyes but nodded my head in agreement. This whole conversation was pointless.

"Do you admit that you feel an attraction toward me?"

"Well yes, Alexandur, I do have eyes and you are a fine-ass man," I replied sarcastically.

"Before last night, were you thinking about being with me?"

I took my time nodding my head because I did not want to admit the truth aloud.

"Kenya, I never hid who I was to you. You are not mad because I am a monster. You are mad because the monster in me killed somebody you did not want to die. The harsh reality of life is that people are meant to fucking die. Why should I feel bad for killing people who have crossed me or my family in some kind of way? I am not an emotional person, but for you I will be. For you, I will make sure you never have to want for anything, and you are always protected for the rest of our lives. The truth is staring you in the face, but you are refusing to see it. Listen to me when I say this, sotie, you are either going to be with me or you are going to be with me. There are no other options. The only thing I ask in return is for your loyalty. You are my woman; you should not have other men in your face. If they do not understand that then they die, simple. As long as you understand that, then we should not have a lot of these minor disagreements."

He was twisting everything and making me question my own logic.

Frustration got the best of me, and I felt tears forming in my eyes. I was so tired of crying. It made me feel like a weak ass bitch and that is something I am not. Alexandur reached out and wiped the tears that had fallen with his hand. Silence surrounded us and he sat quietly while I sorted through my thoughts and emotions.

"How do I know you will not kill me? And what about your loyalty? I will not be with a cheater."

"If I ever kill you, I will have to kill myself and I do not plan on dying anytime soon. Will I hurt you, yes, and most of the time you will enjoy it, but I will never hurt you more than you can handle. As far as the other question, I do not want anybody else but you. Trust me, I have fucked a lot of women but none of them ever made me think about them. You are the only one for me."

"Your words sound so pretty but your actions do not align. We have not even gone out on a date yet, but you call me wife as if that endearment holds any weight without actions."

He was quiet for a few seconds before nodding his head.

"I apologize. Being in a relationship is new for me and there are times when I will mess up. After we eat lunch, may I take you out to see a show and then to have an eloquent dining experience?"

Alexandur's accent made some of his words sound funny, and I laughed. Maybe I wasn't the good person I thought I was. Maybe I was about to make the biggest mistake of my life. *Maybe, maybe, maybe...*

"Yes, Alexandur, I would love to, but can we go later tonight? The sun and my skin do not get along and I don't want to break out."

He smiled at me before standing up to place a soft kiss on my lips.

"Of course. We can leave at seven; the sun will be gone by then. Is there anything else I can do for you before we leave?"

My eyes went to the wall where my phone still lay cracked. I knew my brother had tried to call or text me.

"Can we get my phone fixed while we are out?"

His eyes followed mine before walking over to pick up my iPhone.

"You will have a replacement within an hour," he replied before walking out of the room. I waited until I was sure he had made it back to the kitchen before jumping up to see if the door was unlocked. I twisted the doorknob and smiled. He had set me free.

Alexandur

Kenya and I enjoyed lunch together. I think she now accepts the fact that we are together, and I am never letting her go. After lunch, I sent Hero out to get her a new iPhone 15. She was on a prepaid plan but I am having her added to my plan so I can handle the bill. When we finished eating, she told me she was about to take a bath and relax until it was time for us to go on our date. Now I am sitting in my office at home making plans for tonight. Bacchanalia is my favorite restaurant. Normally, it is booked out several months in advance, but if you were one of the restaurant's highest paying customers the owner will make sure to accommodate you accordingly. My family happened to dine there and hold meetings there quite often. We also let them get a great discount on the wholesale price of the wine they purchased from us. Not only was the food superb but the restaurant was named after the festivals of Bacchus. Bacchus was the Roman god of wine, agriculture, and fertility. Mythology was my favorite lesson to learn. In my opinion, mythology taught more about the study of the conscious and unconscious behaviors of humans and nonhumans more than psychology. People could learn a lot from mythology if they listened to the stories to understand. I called the restaurant, and after giving my name the reservations were made. Getting tickets to the show was easy. It only took a few minutes online and they were bought.

After the night and day we had, I felt like Kenya deserved something nice and I needed a way to let people know she was Mafia affiliated until I could talk her into getting a tattoo. Brown and Co. Jewelry would do an exceptional job and have what I wanted ready within the next week. I called the store and asked to speak to the manager. I told the manager what I wanted, and he suggested a yellow-gold eagle silhouette diamond necklace. It will have approximately 3.17 carats and only cost me twenty-five thousand dollars including the fee for personal delivery. My iPhone dinged before I could set it back down on my desk.

Constatin: Five minutes away.

Me: In office, come on up.

In exactly seven minutes I heard footsteps approaching. The door to my office opened and in walked Constatin, Roman, and Kofi.

"Good afternoon, come on in and have a seat."

"Somebody is in a good mood, hmmm," Constatin replied.

"Is my sister up? I been calling her phone, but it is not working," Kofi asked me.

"Yes, she is up. She was in our room taking a bath before I came in here. She got upset at me and threw her phone, but Hero is at the store getting her a new one right now."

Kofi looked at me crazy before him and Constatin laughed. Roman did not join in with them but he did have a smirk on his face.

"Enough small talk. Why are y'all here?" I asked them. We did not have a meeting scheduled and Kofi had some papers in his hands.

"I broke through the security system protection on the computer, but it was mostly useless. I was able to find messages between him and whoever paid him to betray y'all," Kofi stated.

"Interesting. Zack claimed he betrayed us because his

daughter was threatened, but he did not mention anything about a payment," I replied.

"In the messages, the person who paid him keeps repeating that 'they' had plans and would do anything to make sure everything went as planned. I believe at least two people are working together instead of just one. As far as whether Zack was really threatened or not, it did not happen in their messages, but it could have been done personally. The messages did not give off stranger vibes, but I brought you a copy to look at them."

Kofi handed me the papers when he finished speaking. I quickly scanned the papers before frowning.

"Did you trace this number?" I asked Kofi.

"Yes, it was from a burner phone and the phone is no longer being used."

"How do we figure out who the hell it is after us then?"

"I went through Zack's financial transactions, and he received a two-million-dollar deposit from a Swiss bank account. The name on the Swiss bank account was just a shell corporation that led to another shell corporation that led to another shell corporation. Whoever is behind this is going to great lengths to hide their identity. Using the Swiss bank account was a smart move in some ways and not so smart in other ways. If you are trying to keep the United States from having access to your money then a Swiss account is the way to go, but Swiss accounts are traceable if they are traced when a transaction is happening."

"The next time the person uses that Swiss bank account to make a purchase, he will be able to track them," Constatin stated.

I sat back in my office chair to think. Most criminals had money in some kind of Swiss bank account. I had a couple of them myself, but I didn't use them unless I was making an international transaction that cost millions, and even then, I would send the payment in some kind of cryptocurrency.

"Do you think we will know who the traitors are before you take over as the Nasu?" I asked Constatin.

"Yes, I do. My guess would be that the main goal for whoever is behind all this is to take over the Romanian Mafia. If I am correct, they will increase their attacks, because they know once I take over it will be harder to take us three down."

"When I find out who it is, they are going to wish the thought of a takeover never entered their mind," I said.

"Da (Yes), we will go on a murder spree," Roman inserted.

It got quiet for a second, all of lost in our own thoughts. My mind wandered to Tree and Hero. They have been with me for years and I never had to question their loyalty. Kofi said there were two people working together though, so I could not completely rule them out. Both of my brothers had two bodyguards, perhaps it is one of theirs. If it is Tree and Hero, I will make them watch me kill everybody they love before slaughtering them.

"Mama said you are marrying Kenya. Is that true?" Constatin asked me.

"You and Mama gossip like old ladies, but yes, that is true. She will be my wife one day soon, but we will wait to have kids until after you take over and have an heir."

"Brother, you don't have to do that."

"Nonetheless, I will. Now get out and take Kofi back with you. I am taking Kenya on a date tonight."

"One last thing before we leave. The next shipment is set to sail out in exactly two weeks. Roman and I will fly out to check on it this time."

Before I could respond, Kofi turned to look at Constatin.

"Can I go with you two?"

Constatin was quiet for a minute before responding.

"We shall see. If my brother says he is marrying your sister then he will keep his word, which makes you family. Family business is Mafia business, but I am not sure you are ready. Our life is dangerous."

"Let me stop both of you now. I don't want to hear the rest of this conversation, because if Kenya asks me, I am telling her everything that was said, and something tells me she doesn't want Kofi getting even deeper involved with us."

Kofi got quiet, confirming my suspicions.

Constatin nodded his and they all stood up to leave. I watched as they walked out of my office while thinking about Kofi's request. When Constatin becomes Nasu he can make Kofi a capo if he wants to, but Kofi will need to prove to Constatin that he can handle our lifestyle before Constatin makes such a huge decision.

Kenya

It was almost time for our date, and I was nervous. Alexandur had disappeared into his office for most of the day and he just recently returned. During that time, I bathed and then moved my items from the room next door into Alexandur's room. Alexandur and I were moving at a fast pace. Tonight at dinner, I will tell him that we need to slow down and take baby steps. In two weeks, that man came into my life and changed everything. I glanced in the mirror at myself again. Because we were going to the movies first and then dinner, I decided against wearing a long dress. Instead, I put on a medium-length, nude-colored dress that fit tight against my breasts but flared out at the bottom. On my feet were the most expensive pair of black heels I owned. I believe I paid almost two hundred dollars for them. My hair was twisted out and my curls were bouncy and full. I decided to do a natural beat on my face and topped it off with some Arabian perfume I got from the TikTok shop.

"Are you ready?" Alexandur asked. He walked up behind me and wrapped his arms around my stomach. He is the only person I know who would wear a suit to the theaters.

"I am. What movie are we going to see?"

"*Bad Boys 4*," he replied.

"Alexandur, have you even seen *Bad Boys* 1-3?"

"Nu (no)."

"Did you choose that movie because I am Black?"

"Yes, and because I like action movies. When we have kids, they will be biracial. I want them to know both Black and Romanian culture. The only way I can ensure that is by learning more Black culture myself."

Yes, it was time to go, because talking about kids after only being together for one day was insane. Then again, I was dating a very insane man. Either way, kids are not something we will be discussing right now.

"Let me grab my purse and we can head downstairs."

He gave me a look to let me know he knew I was changing the subject, but I did not care. Ten minutes later we were in the back seat of Tree's truck leaving out of the driveway.

Bad Boys 4 was the best movie I had seen in years. It was so funny and full of action. I laughed until my stomach hurt. After we left the movies, we went straight to the restaurant so we would not miss our reservations. Everybody in Atlanta knew about Bacchanalia, it was the most exclusive restaurant in the whole town. Alexandur had to have paid a lot of money to get last-minute reservations. When we walked inside the restaurant a few people stared at us as we walked past them. I looked over at Alexandur to see if he noticed the people watching us, but he did not glance back at any of them. We were seated as soon as Alexandur told the waitress his name. A server approached us to get our drink order and asked what bottle of wine would be having with dinner. Alexandur replied and the server walked away.

"Is the wine you ordered good?"

"Of course, sotie. It is one of our highest-selling wines. The majority of the high-end restaurants serve it."

Alexandur and I talked so much about his illegal business that I was lost when it came to legal business.

"Can you tell me more about what you do at Bucur Wine International?"

"I am over the Protective Service Department. Anything dealing with the company's security, I handle. I personally train, evaluate, and hire any security detail that works in our building. I also make sure equipment such as cameras and alarms are working efficiently."

"Do you enjoy it?"

"Yes, I do. I feel like it is my responsibility to make sure my family and the employees are safe. I take what I do seriously because I do not want to be caught off guard at work. Plus, my grandfather worked hard to build his company up from the ground. One day our kids will work there too."

Here he goes, talking about kids again.

"Do you think we are moving fast? We basically live together, and you keep talking about marriage and kids as if we have been together for years."

He chuckled before answering my question.

"If I had my way, we would have gotten married this morning. Are you on birth control?"

"Wait. What? You say some crazy ass shit. Who marries somebody they have only been in an official relationship for one day? Do you take psychotic medicine?"

"No. I am not psychotic; I am a monster. Are you on birth control?"

"Some people would say calling yourself a monster is a sign of psychosis, and yes, I have the Mirena in my arm."

"Good, we must wait until after my brother becomes Nasu and produces an heir before we have kids. Well, we do not have to, but we will."

"I'm surprised you don't already know I am on birth control, and is producing an heir a requirement to become the Nasu? If so, who made it a requirement?"

I know I was full of questions, but I wanted to know everything I could about the man that I might or might not end up marrying.

"Medical is only included in a background check if it is directly asked for, and the Mafia has a board of leaders that make decisions for the greater good of all the Mafias."

My life had officially become a Tyler Perry play. The server approached our table, ending our conversation. He gave us our drink and the bottle of wine Alexandur ordered. I decided to just eat a salad because of the food I ate earlier in the day. Alexandur's order was something that I could not pronounce, but he let me taste it when the server brought it to the table, and it was delicious. The rest of our dinner was spent having casual conversation. Alexandur was easy to talk to because he answered every question bluntly. By the time we made it back to the house, we had drunk two bottles of wine and I was tipsy. On the way up the stairs, I stumbled. Alexandur scooped me up in his arms and carried me the rest of the way to our bedroom.

"Thank you," I told him. I reached up to place a kiss on his lips before wiggling in his arms for him to let me down. Instead, he carried me to the bed and reached down to remove both of my high-heeled shoes for me.

"Do you want to take your shower first or should I?" I asked him. Alexandur looked at me and I noticed his eyes getting darker.

"Stand up and take off all your clothes."

I should have been scared but the lure of danger had me feeling excited. I stood up and started taking off all my clothes. When a pair of black thongs was the only thing left on my body, I slid them down slowly. Alexandur watched as I carried the thongs in my hand to where he stood.

"Open your mouth," I demanded softly. He complied and opened his mouth wide. I stuffed my thongs inside of his mouth and watched him close his mouth back shut. He sucked on them for a few moments before taking them out of his mouth and tossing them on his dresser.

"Can you handle my monster?"

He watched me closely as I turned my head to peer at him before I understood what it was he was saying.

"You are about to hurt me?" I asked him for clarification.

"Badly. You can scream. You can cry. But you cannot run from me."

I could feel my pussy essence leaking from inside of me and coating my pussy lips.

"I can handle your monster," I whispered.

He grabbed me by my neck and pulled me closer to him. We kissed each other passionately, and he grabbed both of my breasts and squeezed them roughly. My nipples hardened in his hands. He twisted both of my nipples until I broke the kiss from the pain coursing through my body.

"Turn around and go lean down on the bed. Hold on to the sheets tight."

My body was shaking but I turned around and put both of my hands on the bed. I heard Alexandur walking around the room and a dresser drawer open and closing. He walked up right behind me and bit the back of my neck until I could feel his teeth piercing through my skin. I screamed and he let my neck go.

"Shouldn't we have a safe word?"

"No. I am going to do what I want, and you are going to take it because you are made for me."

Before I could respond, I heard a humming noise then electricity shot through my lower body. I screamed so loud that I knew the bodyguards had to hear me. My body froze up and I could feel a painful tingling sensation everywhere. The humming sound stopped, and he moved whatever device he used away from my body. The painful tingling sensation started to ease, and I felt my body loosen back up.

"Good girl. Damn, I love it when you scream. Spread your legs wide for me."

He was about to shock my pussy lips off my body. Seconds passed by before I swallowed my fear and did as he asked. Pain turned Alexandur on and I had to trust him to know he would not do anything that would hurt me permanently. I spread my legs wide and grabbed the cover on the bed tight. The humming sound began again, and I felt the object touch my clit. The painful tingling sensation started but this time it was bearable. My legs started to shake, and my vision clouded. The pain was becoming pleasurable. So pleasurable that I moaned.

"Fuck, you are so wet. I can see it on your thighs."

"I'm-I'm," I stuttered before falling forward on the bed. An orgasm so powerful took over my body that I cried from how good it felt.

Alexandur

Kenya lay flat on the bed quivering while I tossed the electric wand on the floor. My dick was harder than it had ever been in my life. My hands quickly unfastened my pants, and I shoved them and my briefs down to the floor. I bit her on the other side of her neck before thrusting my dick deep inside of her. We both moaned. Her pussy was nirvana. She was so tight and wet that I feared I would nut too soon. I pumped in and out of her roughly a few times before I pulled out and dropped to my knees. My face went in between her legs, and I licked up all her pussy essence before letting my tongue slide inside of her.

"Alexandur," she moaned my name softly, causing me to grunt. I tongue fucked her pussy until I felt her quivering on my tongue. Right before she could cum, I slipped my tongue out of her pussy and slipped it inside of her ass. She screamed and squirted on the bed. My tongue slid in and out of her ass before I stood up, turned her over, and thrust my dick back inside of her pussy. I grabbed a handful of her hair while I beat into her pussy relentlessly. Kenya put a leg up on the bed and threw her ass back, meeting me thrust for thrust. Every time she pushed her pussy back against me, I felt her take parts of my dark soul.

"If I cannot have you, no one will. I will never let you go," I moaned before nutting all inside of her.

It took me a couple of minutes to regain complete control of my senses. When I did, I slid my dick from inside Kenya and then went to start the shower for us. I walked back into the bedroom to scoop Kenya up and carried her to the shower. In the shower, we took turns cleaning each other before going out to brush our teeth. Before I left out of the bathroom, she was putting that big hair cloth thing on her head.

"Sotie, what is that and what does it do?"

"It's called a bonnet, and it protects my hair when I sleep."

I nodded my head in confirmation before walking to climb into the bed on the left side closest to the door. Kenya came out of the bathroom a couple minutes after me, and I watched as she crossed the room and got in the bed. I pulled her into my arms and kissed her forehead before I closed my eyes and went to sleep.

Kenya had to work Sunday and I was not happy about it. The only thing that kept me from setting Hooters on fire was she informed me that on Sundays they closed at five p.m. While she was gone, Kofi came back home. I was in the kitchen fixing me some coffee when he walked in.

"What up," he spoke and stuck his hand out for a fist pound. I pounded his fist, and he walked over to have a seat at the kitchen table.

"Kenya should be home at around five thirty."

"I know. She always gets off early on Sundays."

"She works too hard. I do not mind her being independent, but she is running herself into the ground."

"That is why I want her to have a million dollars too. When I get my million, she will not accept any of it from me. She is too stubborn."

"A million dollars is chump change. Kenya is about to marry a billionaire and I will not make her sign a prenuptial agreement."

"Hell naw. Sister or not, it could not be me. You on some simp shit."

What does simp shit mean?

"Does that mean you think I will be a good husband?"

"Yup, something like that, Alexandur."

Kofi was trying hard to hold his laughter in and I felt like I was missing some part of the conversation.

"Speaking of my sotie, you know she doesn't want you to become a capo, right?"

"I am grown now and can make my own decisions."

"It will not be easy, Kofi. Constatin is a real drill sergeant. You will be representing the family and he will not send you out there unprepared."

"I am glad you said that because Constatin mentioned that you have a gun range at the back of your house. Can you teach me how to shoot?"

"Hmmm. You two are sneaky. Kenya is not going to like this, but you are a man now and a man must know how to protect himself. Let me finish my coffee and we can go."

Kofi jumped up and ran to hug me. I did not hug him back, but I felt like he approved of me as a brother-in-law and that would matter to Kenya.

I finished my coffee and took Kofi to my gun range. It had not been used in a few years, but it was still in excellent condition. Surprisingly, Kofi learned how to shoot accurately within the first couple of hours of us being out there. I told him if he were not a genius and Mafia affiliated, he could have joined the army as a sniper. He told me that one day he would find the people who killed his parents and return the favor. I offered to do it for him, but he declined and told me it was personal. At four thirty, we left the gun range and came in the house to wait on Kenya. Kenya was tired when she got home, so I ordered us dinner. My night ended with Kenya on top of me, riding my dick while I choked the shit out of her until we both erupted together.

Kenya

Alexandur and I had fallen into a routine over the last couple of weeks. We got up together and worked out. Then we showered, ate breakfast, and went to work. At night he would fuck me until my pussy was sore and my throat raspy. I kept telling myself not to fall in love with him, but my stupid heart did not listen. Now I'm at work sitting at my desk wondering how I could make an unemotional person like Alexandur fall in love with me back. I decided to pull out my phone and message my best friend. Ari and I hadn't talked as much lately because she was doing her last semester of clinicals before she graduated college and took the nursing exam. This was important though, and I needed my best friend's advice.

Me: Best friendddddddd.

Ari: Stranger Danger, I KNOW this not who I think it is??

Me: Girl, don't play with me. My man got a private jet, don't make me pop up.

Ari: Bitch bye, I know you lying. Man? Since when?? And I don't know??? Yeah, you capped out.

Me: No I'm not bestie, I put it on you that I'm being for real.

Ari: Girl please, don't make me jump through this phone and whoop yo' ass. You would never lie on me so what's tea?

Me: Whew, my life has been insane this last month, but long story short, I am in love with a difficult man.

Ari: LOVE! Somebody done stole my best friend phone now they playing games. Whoever this is, just now when we catch your ass it's on and popping.

Me: Ain't nobody stole my phone Jakeisha, you just crazy as hell.

Ari: Dang, so it really is you. Only three people know my middle name and one of the three is six feet under. Okay, let's slow down. When did you meet this man and are y'all in a relationship-relationship?

Me: A month ago, and yes, I know it sounds crazy but he has already told me he is going to marry me soon.

Ari: You damn right you sound crazy. Crazy as hell. If you do not leave that man alone with his lifetime-sounding ass.

Me: I cannot leave him alone, it is against the rules. Plus, he is kind of dangerous and a billionaire. There is no leaving him. I do not want to leave him anyway. I am in love with him, but he has problems expressing emotions in a healthy manner. How do I get him to say he loves me?

Ari: You knew to text me this bullshit while I was in class because bitch, is you on drugs? Do not even bother responding because clearly you done lost your damn mind. I am booking my plane ticket today. As soon as I take my exam in a few weeks, I'm teleporting my ass to Atlanta. My best friend done fell in love with a scammer, but I got a scam for his ass as soon as I touch down.

Ari had me laughing so hard because I knew she was dead serious. I began typing a response, but somebody knocked on my office door. I closed out of our messages and put my iPhone on the desk.

"Come in," I yelled out.

"Um, Ms. Kenya, there are two police officers here to see you," one of the waitresses said before the officers in question came barging into my office. One of the officers was a short black man with a gold tooth in his mouth and the other was a white officer about average height with a beer belly.

"Thank you, sweetie," I replied to the officers and waited until she closed the door to address the officers.

"Good morning Officers, how may I help you?" I asked them, confused.

"Yes ma'am, can you tell us where you were on Friday three weekends ago around twelve in the morning?" the black officer asked.

Oh SHIT. I knew this would come back to bite me in the ass.

"I'm pretty sure I was at home in bed at that time," I replied.

"That's funny, because your neighbor said she hadn't seen you in over a month," the white officer stated.

"Oh, my apologies, I have been staying with a friend for the last month. That's where I was."

"Ma'am, does it look like we are here to play games with you. Chris Wilkins's wife said he got involved in a bar fight protecting you a week before he disappeared, now you can't remember where you were when you are the last person to see him alive," the white officer fussed at me.

"Sir, I am not playing any games. I told you where I was. I didn't even know he had disappeared, I thought he just quit."

"Stand up, we are taking you downtown for questioning. Maybe that will help jog your memory."

My heart dropped and I reached to pick up my phone to call Alexandur, but the Black officer snatched it out of my hand while the white officer grabbed my arm to yank me up. They put me in handcuffs and escorted me out of the restaurant like a criminal. I had never been so embarrassed in my whole life. The only thing that kept me from losing my shit was Tree standing outside his truck on the phone.

Alexandur

"Kenya is on her way to jail."

I looked at my phone to make sure I was not hearing things, but Tree was indeed on the other line.

"What do you mean she is on the way to jail? What the fuck for?" I yelled. I stood up from my desk and grabbed my suit jacket.

"I do not know. The officers that took her were not any of ours and they were being rough with her."

I hung up the phone and stormed out of my office. Mrs. Martin called my name, but it was best for me and her that I keep moving. When I got on the elevator I tried to calm down, but I ended up punching the wall. Kenya's necklace was supposed to be ready last week, but the manager told me he needed more time. He promised to include a matching set of earrings for free for the delay. Her jewelry will be personally delivered to her job tomorrow. Regardless of if she had the golden eagle chain on or not, somebody was about to pay for touching my woman. It took me five minutes to make it to the employee parking lot and when I did, Constatin and Roman stood beside my car waiting for me.

"Tree called Tom and Tom called Father, he is already on the way to the precinct." I hit the unlock button on my key fob and got inside my car. My brothers jumped in my car with me, and I sped the hell up out of there.

"Brother, I know you are mad, but let me do the talking when we get there," Constatin stated.

"Your woman was not the one dragged out of her place of business in handcuffs. Tree said they were rough with her, so I am going to be rough with them."

Constatin took a deep breath but did not reply to my statement. I was doing eighty in a fifty, fuck a ticket, racing to the police station. When I pulled in front of the police station, Tom's car was parked across the street, which meant my father beat me here. I opened my car door and got out. In my background, I could hear my brothers getting out, but I did not wait on them. Atlanta police station was packed with police officers and the people they arrested. I walked past them all and toward the police chief's office.

"Excuse me, sir. Sir. SIR! You can't go in there. He is in an important meeting," the police chief's secretary was yelling at my back. I opened the police chief's door and strolled inside.

"Mr. Bucur, I was just explaining to your father that I have no idea what is going on. The only woman who was just recently arrested is a Black woman who worked at Hooters. I know that is not who you are looking for, so there must be some kind of miscommunication."

"Brother, wait," Constatin said as I advanced toward the police chief's desk. I slapped the police chief as hard as I could, before grabbing him by his neck and pulling his incompetent ass up out of his chair.

"Where the fuck is my woman! Take me to Kenya now!" I yelled.

"Son, let him go." My father and Tom started pulling on me. I let the police chief's neck go and dropped him on the floor, before turning and punching Tom in his nose.

"SON!" my father yelled out.

"Father, I would advise you to let my arm go. Everybody's

calling my name, but nobody is showing me where the hell Kenya is in this filthy ass building."

My father shot a deadly glare at me, and I returned it. He nodded his head before letting my arm go. I squatted down to where the police chief still lying on the floor gasping for air and grabbed him by his cheeks.

"The Black woman you spoke of is my woman. If you are still on this floor by the time I reach for my gun, I will be snatching your woman up out of her bed and dragging her out of your home tonight." His face turned bright red before he rushed to his feet.

"Mr. Bucur, sir, we did not—"

"You are wasting time, and my brother has a short fuse. Witnesses are the only reason you are still alive, take us to my sister-in-law," Roman angrily stated, before the police chief could waste any more time trying to explain the actions of his police officers. Without another word, the police chief walked past us and out of his office. I followed closely behind him. He walked past his front desk and down a hallway before stopping at the third door on his right.

"Just admit that you know where Chris is, and you can use the phone," the white officer was saying as we entered. The police chief tried to clear his throat to get his attention, but I had already grabbed a handful of his hair and slammed his face into the table.

"What the fuck!" The other officer jumped up, but Roman had already pulled his gun out and pointed it at the officer.

"Sotie, baby, are you okay?" I asked Kenya.

"Yes, did Tree call you? I tried to, but they snatched my phone out of my hand."

"It's okay baby, it's all over now."

"Can I go? My hands are still handcuffed."

"The treatment of this young lady will be reported to our lawyer. She should have never had handcuffs put on her in the first place, because she was not under arrest."

"Yes sir, Mr. Bucur," the police chief replied to my father

before walking over to take the handcuffs off Kenya. The Black officer's eyes got big when he heard our last name, before looking at me with fear. Kenya stood up and stretched her arms and legs out and then walked over to me. I pulled her into my arms and pressed a soft kiss on her lips.

"This will never happen again, sotie. I am going to make sure of it."

Kenya nodded her head, but I could see the doubt in her eyes. Those motherfuckers had my woman thinking they were invincible, but I could not wait to show her just how little they really meant.

"We need to talk, and your mother said it's time for her to meet her daughter-in-law," my father said as we walked out of the door.

"Neither one of you needs to go back to work today. We will ride with Father back to the job. You two go on home."

I nodded my head at Constatin, but I ignored my father. He was going to try to tell me to wait before I made my move so things could die down, but things had gone too far. There will be no waiting.

Outside of the police precinct, I opened the passenger side door for Kenya and waited for her to get in the car before I closed it back. By the time I sat down in the driver's seat, Kenya was already buckled in and ready to go. I closed my door and hit the start button on my car.

"What made them come arrest you?" I questioned.

"Chris's wife told them that he had gotten in a bar fight protecting me a few weeks ago and suggested I was the last person to see him alive. One of them asked me where I was three Fridays ago, and I replied that I was at home. They accused me of lying, because they went to my old house and the neighbor told them I had not been there in a month. I was trying to explain to them that I have been staying with a friend and that is what I mean by home, but one of them snatched my phone, while the other snatched me out of my chair. They arrested me and took me to the station. Alexandur, what do I do if they come back? And I need to get back to work. I am going to end up losing my job."

"You do not have to worry about being questioned about Chris anymore, Kenya. That was my fuck up. I should have passed his name over to the police chief and he would have never allowed his officers to investigate. As far as your job goes, you will still have your job tomorrow if you want it. Why you work there anyway when you are about to marry a billionaire is pure stubbornness."

"When I have money to waste in my bank account, then I will think about not working as much, but until then, I would like to keep my job."

"Do you want me to add you to my main bank account or to transfer money into yours?"

"I hope you do not think I'm so independent that I would turn down free money. You can do either one, thank you."

I chuckled before shaking my head. Inside I was still boiling hot, but I did not want Kenya to see how close I was to letting my monster out. The drive home took an hour because I took the long way to let the opera music I had on work its magic on my temper. When I did park in my normal spot in front of my house, my monster was not calm, but he was patient. I got out my car and walked around to open the door for Kenya. Together we walked in the house holding hands.

"Kenya," Kofi said softly before pulling his sister into his arms and hugging her tight. Everything happened so fast that calling her brother slipped my mind. It was obvious by how tight he was holding her though that he knew. One of my brothers had to have called and told him because the bodyguards would not have done so without my permission.

"Have you eaten?" I asked Kofi when he finally let his sister go.

"No, not really. I have been on the computer working all morning."

"How about I take you two out for dinner tonight? There is

this new restaurant downtown that I have been wanting to try out."

"Sure," Kofi said and then shrugged his shoulders.

"Go get ready. We can leave here in an hour. That will give us all the time we need to shower and get dressed. Tree and Hero both will go as well, to watch over us tonight."

"Cool. See y'all then," Kofi replied before giving his sister one more hug and walking toward the stairs.

"What are you up to?" Kenya asked me as soon as Kofi walked away.

"Can I not feed my woman and brother-in-law?" I replied.

Kenya's suspicions were correct. We were only going to dinner so that I could get her drunk enough to fall right asleep when we got back home. I did not have time for her to be trying to beg me not to kill somebody tonight when she found out I was leaving. It would only lead to a minor disagreement between us. An hour later we all left the house. Kofi decided to ride with the bodyguards instead of with me and Kenya. He was up to something, but I did not want to make assumptions until he presented me with his findings.

Dinner went by smoothly, but Kenya would only drink two glasses of wine. Even after I ordered a second bottle, she would not indulge. I did not want to make my plans obvious so as soon as she yawned, I told them it was time to go. On the ride home she fell asleep in the car and instead of waking her up when we pulled into the yard, I carried her to the house. In our bedroom, I gently slipped her in on her side of the bed and walked into my closet to change.

"Where are you going?" she asked when I walked back out of the closet. Kenya was up and sitting on the edge of the bed waiting patiently for me.

"To kill a few people, I will be back soon."

There was no point in hiding the truth from her anymore.

"I want to go."

"Nu (no)."

"Alexandur, it is not like you have not killed in front of me already. Let me go with you please?"

"You are not going to like what I am going to do."

"I promise to behave. They made me feel low and powerless today. I will not stop whatever it is you plan on doing."

Letting her go with me or locking her in the room were my only two choices. I looked Kenya in the face, and she stared back at me with anger in her eyes.

"Hurry up and go change, we have two stops to make."

Tonight was all about teaching a lesson. The officers who arrested Kenya had to know by now they crossed the Romanian Mafia. They would be expecting an attack, but their time to die would not be tonight. Kenya went in her closet and came back out dressed in black like me. She was so beautiful that I wanted to bend her over and fuck the shit out of her if we had the time.

"Come on, sotie."

Kenya nodded her head and then followed behind me. Hero was waiting for me at the bottom of the stairs as expected.

"Here bossman, take this vehicle. Everything you need is in the back," he replied while handing me a set of car keys. It was obvious he was stunned to see Kenya with me by the way he was staring at her. If he stared at her one second longer though, I would have slit his throat. He must have sensed the danger in the air because he blinked and then turned to look at me. He then dropped his head quickly and got the hell away from me.

"Your eyes have that crazy look in them," Kenya laughed as we walked out of the door. My darkness was rubbing off on her and it was intoxicating. Outside of the house was an older model, brown Ford pickup truck. I walked to the passenger side and opened the door for Kenya and then walked around to the driver's side and got in. The truck was so old it made a rattling noise when I crunk it up. It was perfect for tonight's mission.

"If anybody ever asks, we left the restaurant and stayed home all night."

"Okay."

Kenya's voice sounded different, but when I looked at her, she gave me a genuine smile. *Is she turned on?*

The ride got quiet, and we enjoyed the slight breeze blowing in from the windows outside. Fall will be here in a couple of months. Kenya told me that was her favorite season.

"Where are we going?" Kenya finally asked.

"To a warehouse downtown. It is owned by one of our lower-ranking soldiers named Pucci. Pucci and I are well acquainted with one another, and I knew I could trust him to do a pickup job for me."

"He picked up the two officers for you?"

"No, the officers will die, but not tonight. The white officer's name is Steven Hall and the Black officer's name is Quan Miller. They both are downtown in a run-down hotel with their wife and kids, scared that the Mafia is on the way to kill them. The police chief told them to book the hotels under their wife's name and they would be safe until he had time to sort this out, but the truth is he set them up. He wanted them in the same spot at a remote location so it would be easier for me to kill them. The police chief believes by offering his officers' heads on a platter, that he will not be held accountable for their actions. He is also a dead man walking, but I will not be the one killing him. Anytime my father has to make a personal appearance to reprimand somebody, he kills them for wasting his time."

"If Steven and Quan are not the ones dying tonight, then who did Pucci pick up?"

"Steven's parents mean the world to him. His father is a retired cop and he followed in his father's footsteps just to make him proud. Quan has an okay relationship with his parents, but they are not his world. His sister is the person he cares the most about. She basically raised him."

"You are about to kill three people?"

Why her voice sounded surprised, I didn't understand. I am only killing one more person than what she assumed.

"Correct. When you fuck with mine, I fuck with yours. You

are the most important person in my life besides my mama, and disrespect will not be tolerated."

She leaned back in her seat and got quiet. The ride to the warehouse was not long. It only took us about twenty-five minutes to get there because Atlanta traffic was lighter at night. When I pulled into the warehouse only one car was there as I requested. I parked the truck and got out. After opening Kenya's door, I grabbed her hand and escorted her inside the warehouse. The warehouse was empty with only four people inside it. Three out of the four had a black bag over their heads,

"Alexandur, all three of them are here like you requested," Pucci stated when we walked up beside him. He looked over at Kenya and back at me, wishing for an introduction, but Kenya was my business, not his.

"Did you get the items I requested?"

"Yes. They are on the tray right there and the gasoline is in the jug on the floor over there."

I nodded my head and walked over to pick up the knife. Pucci went and removed the black bags from over all three of the people's heads.

"Take the tape off too. I want to hear them scream," I told him. He nodded his head in confirmation and did what I asked.

"Why am I here?" Steven's father asked.

"Your son disrespected somebody very important to me," I replied.

"Look, I do not know any of you people. You have the wrong person. Y'all can just let me go and I will not say anything," Quan's sister begged.

"You are right, you didn't do anything, but Quan did."

When I mentioned her brother's name, her eyes got big.

Done with the conversation, I walked over to pick the knife up. I decided to kill Quan's sister first, to make Steven's parents watch.

"Please. Please!" she begged, as I approached her, but she only fed my monster's ego with her cries.

I walked behind her and pulled her head back. Slowly, I cut her from ear to ear, killing her swiftly. I took a few steps to the left where Steven's mother had her eyes closed praying. I put my hand over her mouth to silence her and plunged my knife into her stomach repeatedly.

Kenya made a small whimpering sound, but I did not turn to look back at her.

"You are not going to get away with this. I have buddies on the force who are going to find out who you are and kill you!" Steven's father screamed.

"Tsk, tsk, tsk. If your buddies are police officers, they aren't supposed to administer any kind of illegal justice. I despise people who use and abuse their job title," I replied, before plunging my knife into the side of his head. I took the knife out and stabbed him in the same spot over and over until I heard Kenya call my name.

"Yes, sotie?" I asked her.

"That's enough Alexandur, they are all dead."

"It was not enough. If I could, I would bring them back alive to kill them over and over again for disrespecting you. Go sit in the truck. I will be out soon."

"No, what are you about to do?"

"Toss gasoline on their bodies and all over this warehouse and set it on fire."

She didn't reply, but I heard her footsteps and then a door slamming shut. Women. They were so difficult.

"Thank you, Pucci, for your assistance. The payment will include enough to buy you a new warehouse."

Pucci walked over to shake my hand before leaving. I pulled a handkerchief out of my pocket and wiped the knife off and then used the handkerchief to toss it on the floor so it would not have my prints on it. The handkerchief went back into my pocket before I picked the gas jug up and tossed gasoline on all three of the people I just killed. I then tossed gasoline around the warehouse until I made it to the door. The empty gasoline jug was thrown inside the warehouse right before I pulled the handkerchief back out of my pocket and a lighter. I lit the handkerchief on fire and slung it in the warehouse. Crackling and popping sounds could be heard when I got back inside the trunk. After cranking the truck up and backing out, I waited a few seconds to confirm the building was on fire before pulling out and driving away. I decided to take the long way back home so we could enjoy the night breeze again.

Kenya

The ride back home was a silent one. My mind was a puzzle, and I could not figure out how I ended up with so many missing pieces. I should feel fear right now. I should feel disgusted. My parents loved one another deeply and I never felt neglected as a child. There was no rational explanation I could find for why, out of all the billions of people in this world, I loved Alexandur so much that I was willing to accept him completely. Nobody is perfect, everybody has flaws, but Alexandur's flaws are unorthodox. The man I was in love with had a monster living inside of him who enjoyed taking other people's lives. My thoughts continued to run rampant in my mind the whole way home. Hero was waiting by the door for us when we walked in to get the keys to the pickup truck. After he got the keys, he wished us both goodnight, but I was too far in my head to respond. Slowly, I ascended the stairs and walked into the room. It was not until Alexandur asked me the dumbest question that I mentally tapped back into the reality around me.

"Are you plotting your escape from me in your head? Is that why you are so quiet?"

I stared at him like I would a toddler throwing a temper

tantrum. He was obviously just cranky to ask a dumb ass question like that.

"I just watched you brutally murder three people, and you believe I am thinking about trying to escape you? No, Sherlock Holmes, I am trying to figure out what in the hell is wrong with my brain."

"Why do you think something is wrong with your brain?"

"Because I care about somebody I shouldn't, and I find the psychotic ass things he does attractive when I should be scared for my life."

"I told you already the answers you seek are staring you in the face. We are meant to be together sotie, stop trying to make sense of something neither one of us had parts in planning. Everything is not meant to be understood. Change what you can and accept the things you cannot change. You being with me is something you cannot change, accept it so we can enjoy our life together."

"Alexandur, I have accepted it which is why I think my brain is fragmented," I replied sarcastically.

"No, you think your brain is fragmented because my monster makes your pussy wet."

"Exactly," I yelled, glad he was finally understanding that something was wrong with my brain.

He chuckled before grabbing my shirt and pulling me close to him. Our lips joined together, and we took turns licking and sucking on each other's tongue until I stepped back to catch my breath.

"Take my clothes off," he demanded. Slowly, I began removing every article of clothing he had on his beautiful body. Then I took turns biting each one of his nipples.

"Fuck, that felt so good. Take all that shit off and go lay down on the bed."

Hurriedly, I got naked and went and laid on the bed. I could hear Alexandur opening and closing the dresser drawers again and my body trembled with fear and excitement.

Is he about to electrocute my pussy again or something else?

Alexandur walked up to the bed with rope in his hands. He tied my hands and feet to his bedpost. I lay naked with my body spread out like an eagle, wondering what he was about to do to me.

"When I went through your stuff, I found your rose toy. Tonight, I am going to use it on you however many times it takes until you squirt in my mouth."

A buzzing sound floated around the room before he placed the rose toy on my clit.

"Oh my god!" I yelled out, before shaking like a stripper on the first of the month.

Alexandur's crazy ass had my rose toy set on the third setting. It made me cum in ten seconds. The buzzing noise went off and I felt Alexandur running two of his fingers up and down my pussy.

"Good girl. Your pussy is so wet, but I want it squirting."

He slapped his hand down on my pussy hard, causing me to moan. He placed the rose toy back on my clit, but this time it was on the second setting. This setting was my favorite because it took my body a whole minute to cum for it. The other two settings made me erupt so fast that the pleasure faded away as soon as I caught my breath.

"Yessss," I whispered. My toes curled and I could feel my orgasm building in my body. My body started to tremble, and I bit down on my bottom lip in anticipation. Then the buzzing noise stopped.

"What the fuck," I whined. Alexandur didn't respond, but after about thirty seconds the buzzing sound started back. I felt my rose toy go back on my clit and I sighed in relief. My orgasm immediately started back building in my body. I thrust my hips up trying to help my body erupt because this orgasm felt stronger. Tears clouded my eyes, and I moaned out Alexandur's name. My pussy walls began tightening up and I closed my eyes. The buzzing noise stopped again.

"Alexandur, what are you doing? Please stop playing, I need to cum really bad," I pleaded with him.

"Cry for me first." The buzzing sound started back, and he placed my toy back on my clit.

"Ahhhhhhhhhhh!" I screamed because the setting was back on three. My body lifted into the air and I just knew my orgasm was going to hit my body so strong that I would see stars. The buzzing stopped. My whole body was wound up tight begging for a release and Alexandur was playing games. I burst out crying.

"Good girl, you always listen so well."

The buzzing sound started back and this time it was on setting two. Scared to get excited just for him to cut it back off, I held my moans in. My orgasm built again, and I silently prayed that God would show me mercy.

"YESSSSSSS!" I screamed. My body erupted and it felt unreal. Liquid shot out of me, and I felt Alexandur's hot mouth sucking it all up while still holding the rose toy on my clit. It triggered another orgasm so powerful everything went black.

"Ouch." Something was sticking me in my neck, causing me pain. Slowly, I opened my eyes and looked down. Alexandur had his teeth so deep in my neck it felt like I was being pierced by a knife. He didn't let go until I felt small blood drops on my collarbone. He leaned down to lick the small drops of blood up at the same time he thrust his dick inside of me.

"Why does your pussy feel so good?" he asked me, before fucking me harder. I lifted my hips up and grinded against him.

"Yes, baby. Fuck me back," he moaned.

Thrust for thrust, we met each other in the middle, until I felt my body about to erupt again. I didn't even know I could cum so many times in one night, but a few seconds later I was coating his dick with my cum.

"Hmmmm," he groaned before grabbing a hold of my neck and choking me. He fucked me harder to the point that I could no longer fuck him back. All I could do was take it. His hand went back, and he growled before I felt his sperm shooting inside of me. His hand released my throat and I inhaled deeply.

Alexandur climbed off the bed and walked away. He liked to

take care of me after we had sex, so I knew he was starting the shower. A couple minutes later, he walked back into our bedroom and took the ropes off my hands and feet. He scooped me up bridal style and carried me to the shower. As soon as we finished showering and changing the sheets, I climbed into the bed and went straight to sleep.

The next morning, I woke up and we did our normal routine. After breakfast, me and Tree left the house and headed to Hooters. At a little after nine, my iPhone dinged with a notification. I unlocked my phone and a bank notification popped up. Alexandur had just transferred a hundred thousand dollars into my checking account. I cleared the text message notification from my front screen and then logged into my banking app to confirm that I wasn't mistaken. Alexandur was out of his mind.

I sat down at my work desk and contemplated what I wanted to do with my life. If I was being honest with myself, I enjoyed working at Hooters. Most of the waitresses were either single mothers or struggling students just trying to make a way. I felt good knowing I was helping other women succeed in life, even if it was just by being a good manager. Alexandur wasn't going to like my decision, but I wasn't about to leave my job. Maybe if we really did get married, I would consider it, but for right now I was doing what made me happy. Kofi crossed my mind, and I wondered if I should add any money to his bank account. Then I decided against it. I didn't want the money to distract him from figuring this mess out with Alexandur and his brothers. Deep down in my heart, I don't believe that Alexandur would kill me or Kofi, but I honestly couldn't say the same for his brothers. For right now, it was best to only spend what was necessary, until everything fell in place. I got up from my desk and locked the office door, before going out front to get the restaurant ready to open. Hooters opened a couple hours later, and everything was going smoothly. Every now and then I would have flashbacks of Alexandur killing those people last night in my mind, but I would force the images away and focus back on whatever task I was doing. Around three p.m. a gentleman entered the restaurant and asked for me. I was standing beside the bar and watched as one of the waitresses pointed me out. I slipped my hands into my jacket pocket and pulled my iPhone out. After what happened the other day, I didn't know what to expect. Imagine my surprise when the nice gentlemen walked up to me and handed me a jewelry bag.

"Are you sure this is for me?" I asked, puzzled.

"Yes ma'am, if your name is Kenya Jones, then Alexandur ordered this for you a couple weeks ago. I apologize for the delay, and I hope you both are satisfied."

Confused, I smiled and thanked him for the package. We wished each other a good day and he left. As soon as he walked out of the restaurant, I ran to my office. I don't know what was going on with Alexandur. First, he deposited money into my account, and now, I get a delivery in a jewelry bag. My hands shook slightly as I pulled two boxes from the jewelry bag. I decided to open the small box first. Inside the small box were yellow-gold diamond earrings that had to have cost a fortune. The diamond sparkled so bright that if I wasn't careful, I could blind myself. I closed the first box back and opened the big box. I almost dropped the big box in shock. Alexandur was the most contradictive man I had ever met. How could a cold-blooded killer be so sweet to me? In the large box was a yellow golden eagle necklace that matched the yellow eagle tattoo Alexandur had on his neck. I put both boxes back inside the jewelry bag and pulled my iPhone back out to call Alexandur.

"Why are you being so nice to me?" I asked as soon as he answered.

"Kenya, what are you talking about?" he asked in an even tone.

"First, you deposited a whole lot of money into my bank account, and now, I just got a delivery with the most beautiful eagle necklace I have ever seen. What did I do to deserve this?"

Alexandur did not laugh like normal people. When he found something entertaining, he just chuckled.

"You are so funny sometimes, *sotie*. The money I put into your account was not a lot of money. Until we are officially married, I am not giving you a large lump sum of cash because I don't want you to use the money to try to escape from me. As far as the jewelry is concerned, I ordered that a couple weeks ago. If you had been wearing that necklace when the police arrived, they would have known you were Mafia affiliated. Of course, that doesn't excuse the way they treated you."

"So basically, you're saying I did nothing to deserve all of this?"

"Precisely. Kenya, you are my woman. It is my job to treat you with nice things and to provide for you."

"Sorry, I apologize for bothering you while you were at work. I am just not used to receiving this kind of treatment, but I am grateful. Thank you."

Alexandur hung up without saying goodbye. I did not take it offensively though, because it was just the way he was. The only emotion I could get out of him easily was anger and he hated that. I replayed the conversation we just had in my mind and realized the importance of the yellow golden eagle. It was obvious Alexandur wanted me to put it on now so that people knew not to mess with me. The problem with that was it was so expensive I was afraid of getting robbed. Maybe if I just wear it under my shirt until I leave work, I will be fine. Plus, Tree is still outside of my job watching my every move, so I am sure he wouldn't let anything happen to me. I put my jewelry bag inside my office drawer and locked it. I got ready to leave my office and go back to work when my iPhone rang.

"Yes, Alexandur?"

"I forgot to mention, we are taking a trip to Sicily next month so that I can check on some of our wine vineyards. I am unsure how far in advance women need to be notified to shop properly.

"Um, okay, I have my passport," I replied.

"We are taking my father's plane. You don't need it."

Alexandur hung up the phone on me again and I went back to work feeling like I was living in some kind of twilight zone.

Alexandur

"Did I not tell you to stand down?" my father asked me sarcastically. I had avoided coming to my parents' house for the last week, but I missed Mama. Plus, I knew if I didn't show my face soon, Mama would've called.

"Father, are they not still alive?"

"Smart ass, you know what I'm talking about. Who did you get to do it?"

"I haven't the slightest idea what you're talking about, but if I were to do something irrational, I would have gotten my own hands dirty."

Father didn't need to know that I used lower-ranking soldiers to do a pickup job for me. All he needed to know was that I was the one who took those people's lives.

"You boys are going to be the death of me. Y'all are too fucking stubborn, and if that woman is to be my daughter-in-law, you need to make it official. Stop dancing around here calling her your wife when you haven't done as you're supposed to do as a man and claimed her."

Father was right, so I only nodded my head. He turned away from me to look at Constantin.

Have you confirmed with the *ndrangheta* that they have received their package?" my father asked Constatin.

"Yes, I have. I spoke with them directly this morning."

"And you are positive that this young man that you have working for us knows what he is doing?"

"Yes Father, Kofi is extremely intelligent and a fast learner. He will figure out who is behind this. He was the one who changed the location and only informed me and the leader of the ndrangheta where to meet a few hours beforehand. He believes that the people after us are closer to us than we expect."

"Hmmmm, all rats must die," Roman whispered. His outbursts were always so random because the majority of the time he remained quiet.

My mind drifted back to the day when Kofi decided to ride in the backseat with Tree and Hero. I knew he was up to something that day. In due time, the truth will come to light.

"Brother, speaking of Kofi, he is spending the weekend with me again. He thinks I don't know he is secretly getting information on my bodyguards, but I know everything that happens in my home."

All of us have cameras in our home, but Constatin is the only one of us who watches the camera feed every day.

"What did you see on the cameras?" I asked him curiously.

"While the bodyguards are distracted, he picks up their phones and hacks into them."

"Interesting," I replied. My thoughts wandered to Kenya, and I thought about what my father just said. It was time to make things official with Kenya, but the problem was that I didn't know if she was going to say yes or if I would have to force her to say yes. It shouldn't matter to me either way, but it did. Kenya was aware of my desire to marry her. Hell, I call her my wife multiple times a day, but she hasn't called me her sotul (husband) yet. She is still mentally battling with the way she feels for me and what she was taught was socially acceptable. Either way, she will be my wife.

"Let's wrap this conversation up. Kenya loves Mama's cooking, so I am going to her job to take her some of the saramura de crap (carp brine) Mother made today."

"I will meet you there because I want you to go with me to meet the lawyers, but I have to see what Lizzy keeps blowing my phone up about," Constatin stated. Elizabeth abuses the friendship my brother has with her to show off for her friends. I expect nothing less, though, from the daughter of a politician.

Kenya

Today felt like a drag. I had been out on the floor with the girls ever since I left my office two hours ago. Business was slow enough out there now for me to catch up on some paperwork. At least that was what I was supposed to be doing. Instead, I was sitting at my office desk daydreaming about shopping. When I was younger and I would get money for my birthday or good behavior, I would immediately beg my parents to go to the store. My momma would say that my money was burning a hole in my pocket. At that age, I never understood what she meant, but now I get it. Now that I had some money, I was ready to spend it all without thinking.

Girl, that is your money. You can spend it how you want.

The irresponsible voice in my head was trying hard to convince me to go shopping, but I was not going to do it. Instead, I decided to message my best friend.

Me: (screenshot sent)

Ari: Bitch, why that bank account got your name on it?

Me: Because it is mine, duhhhhh.

Ari: Oh Lord, the scammer done got you caught up in some bullshit.

Me: Crazy, he isn't a scammer. His family owns a wine company, you can Google him.

Ari: And will! What's his first and last name?

Me: Alexandur Bucur.

Ari: Please hold one second.

I laughed while waiting on my crazy ass best friend to go snooping. A few minutes later, my iPhone dinged.

Ari: Girl, you did not tell me you were dating a white man, and a fine one at that. Forbes said he and his family are billionaires. Tell my new brother-in-law I said heyyyyyy.

Me: He is Romanian, and I thought you were coming down here to kick his ass.

Ari: You know like I do that if he hurt you, I will whoop his billionaire ass, but don't tell him that. I'm trying to get the hookup with one of his friends.

Me: Ugh, I miss you so much. I cannot wait until you come down here. I'm buying your plane ticket and taking you shopping. You deserve it. I know how hard you worked on getting out of the hood and becoming something that you are passionate about. My best friend is about to be a nurse and a damn good one at that.

Ari: I love you Kenya, you know you the addict and I'm the crack. It's a lifelong addiction baby.

Me: BYE! Hell is too hot to be playing with you, and why I always got to be the addict?

A knock on my door had me closing out of our messages and putting my iPhone down. I could not wait until Ari came to town. I missed the hell out of her.

"Come in," I yelled out.

"Ms. Kenya, there is a man here claiming to be your husband," one of the waitresses peeked her head in the office and spoke.

Alexandur is here? Uh oh, what did I do?

Instead of responding, I slid my iPhone in my pocket and stood up. Alexandur was sitting at one of the tables scrolling on his phone when I walked to the front of Hooters. Frowning, I slowly approached him and sat across from him.

"What's wrong?"

"What do you mean?"

"Um, you never stop by here and you didn't mention coming on the phone."

"Do I need a reason to come see my sofie?"

His voice had gotten deeper when he asked that question.

"No, of course not, I am just surprised that's all."

Alexandur did not respond. He reached down in the chair beside him and brought up a lunchbox.

"You brought me food?" I asked him.

"Mama cooked and I know how much you like trying Romanian dishes. This one has brine and is healthy. She packed it in my old lunchbox."

Awww, sometimes Alexandur was so sweet. The more time I spent with him the harder I was falling in love with him. Before I could respond, a beautiful white woman squealed his name and then threw her arms around him.

"Alexandur, I miss you. We never get to spend any time together anymore."

On second thought, this bleach-blonde, bad-built, butch-body trick had a face that only a mother could love.

"Elizabeth," Alexandur replied without removing her arms from around him. That was all I needed to see. I stood up and walked away before I ended up back in jail. The keys were barely in my office door before Alexandur came barging in behind me.

"You can go back out there with your little girlfriend," I said without turning around.

"Kenya, what the hell is wrong with you? Why did you just leave like that?" he questioned me. I sat down at my desk and picked up another piece of paper to read.

"Kenya, I don't like when you ignore me."

He was issuing a warning, but he could take that warning and shove it right up his and his girlfriend's bleach-blonde ass.

"Get up and get your shit, you are going home now," he yelled.

I put the paper down and picked up another one and read that one.

"How dare you disrespect me?"

"Disrespect you? Be fucking for real, you just let some woman put her arm all around you and I'm the disrespectful one. Now if the situation had been reversed and some man did that to me, he would be dead right now."

"You are correct, I would have killed him before his hands even touched you."

He was so mad his eyes were turning dark, but I was mad too.

"Exactly, now you can go back out there with your little girlfriend like I said and close the door on your way out."

"You will pay for this foolishness. If you had been paying attention, you would have seen Constatin standing behind you. Elizabeth is his best friend and future wife."

"I don't give a fuck if she was the president of the United States of America, you should have never let her touch you," I jumped up and screamed. My body started shaking and my eyes rolled to the back of my head.

"Kenya!" Alexandur screamed, and then I heard nothing.

ALEXANDUR

Systemic lupus erythematous. Lupus. Kenya has lupus and I knew nothing about it. I sat beside the hospital bed staring at the wall. Uncurable. Lifelong illness. She will wake up when her body is ready. All the words the family doctor spoke to me less than an hour ago. Lupus occurs when the immune system attacks healthy tissue and organs. Kenya's body went into a seizure, and she passed out.

"Brother," Constatin tried talking to me, but my brain was only focused on Kenya. I did not even know if I still possessed the ability to open my mouth let alone speak. After pulling her medical records, the family doctor informed me that Kenya had been diagnosed with lupus the same year her parents were murdered.

Tears were a foreign concept to me, and fear was a useless emotion. Yet I found myself fighting back tears because I felt fear. Fear for Kenya. Fear of the unknown. Fear of failure. How can I cure what can't be cured? How can I fight what I cannot see? How can I protect Kenya from the enemy when the enemy lived inside of her? My cheeks felt wet, and a throbbing pain spread throughout my chest.

"Kenya is the strongest woman I know. She will wake up

soon," Kofi said more to himself than anybody else. From the time he entered the hospital room, he had not moved from standing beside the hospital bed holding his sister's hand. He knew about her diagnosis. I thought back to all the times he would tell her that stress was bad or to calm down it was not healthy. How could I miss all the signs when they were right there? I knew I did not deserve Kenya, but I thought I was protecting and providing for her as a real man should. A real man would have noticed something was wrong with his woman. A real man would have not caused the person he cared the most about to stress herself into a seizure. I was only a monster, not a real man.

Time blurred together and I remained staring at the wall. The doctor had come in and checked her vitals and they were good. He said her white blood cell count was low which he believed was the main cause of her lupus flare-up. They were injecting her IV with the necessary antibiotics and steroids her body needed. After the doctor finished relaying that information to me, he left without waiting for a response. One of my brothers must have told him that I was not in the mood for words. The more the seconds ticked by, the more a piece inside of me died. Kenya was the light to my dark. The calm to my chaos. The beat inside of my heart that made me feel alive. I could not live without her.

"It's going on four hours, and you haven't moved or said anything. I am worried, brother. Mama and Father are on the way here," Constatin said. He stood in front of the chair I sat in waiting for a response, but he did not get one. Why couldn't he let just me suffer in peace?

I smelled my mama before I saw her. She always smelled like spring flowers and warm pie right out the oven.

"Fiul (son)," my mama said gently. I turned around to look at her in her face. My cheeks felt wet again and my body fought with the urge to respond to my mama, but I just could not.

"Awww, sweet fiul, Mama is here now." I closed my eyes to let her voice seep into my skin and flow to my brain. A part of me wondered if she was disappointed in me. I did not have to look over at my father to know he saw a broken soldier sitting in front of him, but did Mama see that I was only a man in age, but not in action?

"Can everyone please step out the room so I can speak with Alexandur?" she asked the others softly. One by one, everyone nodded and left us two alone.

Mama wrapped her arms around me and held me tight. On the outside I froze, rigid in response, but on the inside, I felt a small sense of serenity slowly start to build.

"You did good fiul, she is more beautiful than I expected," Mama whispered in my ear. A gasp escaped from my throat, and I slowly wrapped my arms around my mama and cried.

"It is okay, Alexandur. She is going to be okay," my mama repeated over and over while still holding me tight. I am unsure how long we stayed like that, but I knew when I opened my eyes again, I turned my head to check on Kenya. Kenya laid there silently, eyes open watching me.

KENYA

Someone was crying and they sounded so sad. For some reason, the cries caused my heartbeat to jump erratically. Confused, I frowned and then opened my eyes.
Where am I? Is that Alexandur crying?

The room I was in was cold and my bones shivered in response. Alexandur was sitting in a chair, not too far away from me, with his arms wrapped around an older woman. The older woman held him tight, but I could not see her face. I wondered if I was dreaming because the man I knew would not cry, and if he did, something was terribly wrong. Alexandur moved his head and our eyes connected. What was wrong with my man?

"Doctor," Alexandur yelled out. The woman that was holding him let him go and turned to look at me. She looked so much like the man I was in love with that the word Alexandur had yelled out did not register immediately until everybody came rushing into the room I was in.

"Kenya," my brother cried out and then ran to wrap his arms around me. It was at that moment reality hit me and I realized what was going on. My lupus had reared its ugly head and made an appearance.

A doctor that I had never seen before came in and asked me

how I was feeling. I replied that I was feeling okay but tired. Dealing with a chronic illness every day was exhausting. Especially a disease like lupus when the symptoms were unpredictable and hard to explain to the outside world. I remember when I first started getting sick. I would lay in bed all day and my boyfriend at the time, Keith, would fuss because he thought I was just being dramatic. In his eyes, because he could not see that I was physically hurting, he believed that I was not in any pain when that was farther from the truth. So, I learned how to cope in silence. I tried to always eat healthy, and I made sure to walk 10,000 steps a day which was easy to do with the job I had. Every day while I was by myself, I took the medicine that I was prescribed and daily supplements such as vitamin D and fish oil. Unfortunately, flare-ups were a part of having lupus and no matter how much I tried to control them, I couldn't.

Alexandur had not taken his eyes off me, and I wondered if he would change his mind about never leaving me now. That was what happened with my ex. He said I had become too much to handle, and he was too young to be worried about somebody with a "disease." At first, when Keith left me, I hated him for doing so, but now that I am older, I understand his actions better. Things were not like how they are now. When I first got diagnosed, I would get sick back-to-back. Ironically, it was not until Keith left me that I decided to take my life back and make the necessary changes to manage my flare-ups as much as I could.

The doctor asked a few more questions, before informing me that I had to spend at least forty-eight hours in the hospital to get my white blood cell count back up some and then he would release me. Familiar with the process, I thanked him and watched as he walked out of the hospital room. Suddenly, I became aware of how many people were in the room with me. There was Kofi, Alexandur, Constain, Rome, and two more people that had to be Alexandur's parents. My eyes roamed around the hospital room noticing how big it was and how much furniture was inside it.

This could not be a regular hospital room. Hell, it looked more like a hotel suite.

"Hello everybody," I spoke, but my voice was full of fatigue. Everybody responded back and I hated how I could hear the pity in their voices. I did not want people to feel pity for me. One of the ways I coped with my disease was that I reminded myself that it could have been worse. People were battling diseases such as cancer and chronic kidney failure every day. They were the ones who deserved to be pitied, not me.

God, I am so tired.

My body felt drained and keeping my eyes open was becoming a struggle. I decided to let fatigue win. As soon as I closed my eyes, I drifted back to sleep.

Alexandur

The doctor was releasing Kenya today and I needed to step out to make a few phone calls.

"Do not let her lift a finger. If she needs to call for a nurse or doctor, you push the button for her," I ordered Tree and Hero before stepping outside. My brothers and parents stayed for a few more hours the other day but eventually, I talked them into leaving. The only demand they had was that my bodyguards had to remain with me the whole time. I tried getting Kofi to go home with Constatin, but he refused to leave his sister's side and I did not blame him. For the last two days, Kenya mostly slept. We barely said much to each other, but it was because I wanted her to rest, and I was still dealing with feeling like a failure.

When I finished making my phone calls, I stepped back inside the hospital room. Kenya had woken back up and was now sitting up in the hospital bed.

"How long do I have before I am free?" she asked me.

"Not long, we should be leaving in about an hour."

"Am I going home or back to your home?"

What the hell kind of question was that?

I glared at Kenya angrily but quickly adjusted my face.

"The only home you have is with me."

A flash of relief crossed her face, and I frowned.

Did she think I would let her go because of her illness? Nothing would ever make me let her go.

The hour came quickly. Kenya frowned as I pushed her in a wheelchair to the car. She wanted to walk, but I told her she could either get in a wheelchair or I would carry her. Tree had left a few minutes before to pull around to the front entrance of the hospital. He was the one driving us home. Hero and Kofi would be in Hero's car following right behind us.

When we made it home, I carried Kenya bridal style up the stairs.

"Would you like for me to run you a bath?"

"Yes, please."

I laid Kenya down on the bed and went to the bathroom to run her bath. It only took about four minutes for the bathtub to get full. When I went back in the room, I walked over to the bed and bent down to scoop Kenya back up.

"What the fuck. Alexandur, you do realize I can walk, right? You are not about to keep scooping me up like I am a child."

"I care about you because I want to, not because I think you need it."

She glared at me and then rolled her eyes. I sat her down on the bathroom counter and began removing her clothes.

"Wait, you cannot be serious. Are you about to bathe me too?"

"Yes, I am," I replied.

Once I had her naked, I scooped her back up bridal style and carried her to the bathtub. Slowly, I lowered her down into the water. For the next fifteen minutes, I took my time bathing Kenya from head to toe. I knew that she was capable of bathing herself, but I wanted to feel needed by her. No, I needed to fill needed by her. After fifteen minutes, I stood up and got one of our big white towels then walked back over to the bathtub.

"Come on," I said to her gently. This time she acquiesced

without any backtalk. She stepped out of the bathtub, and I wrapped the big white towel around her beautiful naked body.

"Which one of these lotions do you want me to rub on you?"

"Alexandur, why are you doing all of this?"

"Because you are my woman to take care of. Show me which one."

She pointed to the brown lotion bottle that had cocoa butter and shea butter on the label. I went and picked up the lotion and squirted some in my hand and then took my time lotioning her down like I had seen her do plenty of times after her shower.

"I draw the line at you brushing my teeth for me," she said jokingly and gave me a light smile. That was the first smile I had seen in days. I walked back over to the bathroom counter, put the lotion up, and then picked up her toothbrush and toothpaste. She said I could not brush her teeth, but she did not say I could not put the toothpaste on the toothbrush for her. When I finished, I handed her, her toothbrush, and she shook her head in disbelief. Silently, I watched as she brushed her teeth and then rinsed with mouthwash. She put everything back where it went, and then turned around to look at me.

"You can go ahead in the room now. I will be in there in a second."

It was something about the way she said it that rubbed me the wrong way. Her voice suddenly turned sad.

"No. Why can't I stay in here with you until you are ready to go back to our bedroom?"

She hesitated for a minute before I saw her eyes cloud with tears.

"Kenya, just tell me what is wrong. I am not leaving, so you might as well just be honest with me."

"I need to check my hair for bald spots, and I don't want you to witness it."

Tears were streaming down her face rapidly, causing a sharp pain to hit me in my chest.

"Baby. Please stop crying and explain to me what is wrong."

"I'm sorry. I know I shouldn't be crying, especially about my hair when there are more important things to focus on. But when you have had to cut all your hair off just for it to grow a little and then you get another bald spot and have to cut it all off again, you would understand why I am crying. Do you know what it is like having to look in the mirror every day and physically be reminded that you have a chronic disease? That is why I asked you to step out, because I know if I find a bald spot I will cry."

I walked up to Kenya and pulled her into my arms.

"How can I help?" I asked her while holding her tight to my chest.

She looked up at me surprised, before wiping her face.

"Are you sure you want to help?"

I did not respond. I just looked at her like she was crazy.

"It will be easier for you to do it if I was sitting down. On the bathroom counter is a yellow tooth comb and some hair oil named kaleidoscope. Can you grab both and I will show you what I want you to do?"

I nodded my head in confirmation before placing a gentle kiss on her lips. I let her go and got the items she requested. Kenya walked out of the bathroom and went to have a seat on the bedroom floor right in front of the bed. Confused, I frowned at her, unsure of what she wanted me to do next.

"Come sit over me, and I will tell you the next step."

I walked over to the bed and sat down with Kenya in between my legs on the floor.

"I am going to show you how to part my hair. All I need for you to do is take your time parting my hair, section by section, to see if you spot a bald spot. After you part a section, I need you to put a little hair oil on my scalp."

Maybe I bit off more than I can chew, but if this what Kenya needs, then I will try.

"Okay, show me how to do it."

Kenya put the comb and oil in front of her and then lowered her head down. First, she grabbed the comb and used it to part a straight line in the back of her head. She had the majority of her hair in a ponytail at the top of her head, except for that one straight line she just parted. How she knew how to part her hair without looking was a mystery. She then put the comb down and picked up the hair oil. The hair oil had a little applicator attached to the opening of it. She squeezed a little oil in the applicator and then used the applicator to put the oil on her scalp. After watching her do it, I realized it sounded harder than it looked.

"Do you think you can do what I just did?" she asked me.

"Yes, I can do it."

For the next forty-five minutes, I searched her hair for a bald spot and then oiled her scalp. Parting her hair straight was a challenge. My parts look more like zigzag lines, but she said that was okay.

When I finished and told her that she did not have any bald spots, she cried tears of joy. I waited until she was done to help her get dressed and made her get in the bed to rest.

"I am going back to work tomorrow. I can't afford to lose my job," she mumbled.

"No, you are not."

"Just because I have $100,000 in my bank account does not mean I can move recklessly. I will get fired if I do not go."

"And still, you are not going. Plus, you own that Hooters now, they cannot fire you."

"What are you talking about? No, I do not."

"Well technically, you are correct. Technically I own it, but I bought it because I knew you would be worried about losing your job and as a wedding present. Once we get married, I will sign it over to you."

She laughed.

"I have never met anybody so insane, manipulative, and sweet like you."

"Go to sleep, Kenya," I demanded, and she closed her eyes.

Kenya

It has been seven days since I got out of the hospital. I returned to work four days ago and surprisingly, nothing went wrong in my absence. It turns out Constantin had hired a temporary floor manager to work for me the day I got hospitalized. On the outside looking in, one would assume that everything was back to normal. That is why they say when you assume you make an ass out of u and me. Alexandur will not touch me. He goes above and beyond to take care of me in every way but sexually. It is as if I am a family member instead of his woman. For the last two nights, I have gone to bed naked to see if he would attempt to fuck me, and both nights, he would just turn away from me and go to sleep. My mama did not raise a fool, and I recognized the signs because I had been here once before. So, before Alexandur gets the chance to break my heart, I will break my own heart first and leave. That is why on my only day off, I am spending it in the closet, packing my shit. Alexandur claimed he had business to handle today and wouldn't be home until later. What he did not know was by the time he got home, I would be long gone. 120429, I watched him put in the same house code the day I returned home from the hospital. Nothing was going to stop me from leaving today. After I had all my bags packed, I started placing them in the hallway. The Uber I ordered will be here in fifteen minutes. I sat on the bed and scrolled Facebook to waste time.

SLAM.

The bedroom door slammed shut. Frowning, I got up to go to the door to open it back, but I couldn't. I twisted it left and right, but the lock would not budge.

What in the world?!

And then it dawned on me. This motherfucker done locked me in the damn room again. I pounded on the door before getting mad and kicking it. My iPhone rang.

"If you end up back in the hospital because you let your temper get you too worked up, I will handcuff your ass to the bed for a month," Alexandur hissed into the phone.

"You aren't even supposed to be here. Let me the hell out now!" I yelled back.

"You know the rules. Leaving me is against the rules. I have cameras all over the house Kenya, including in our bedroom."

I screamed before hanging up the phone. Alexandur called right back, but I hit the ignore button.

Calm down, Kenya. Calm down.

I did some breathing exercises before I went to sit down on the couch in the corner. The last time he locked me inside the room, he brought me food to eat. Today when he brings the food, I am going to smash the plate right upside his head. Feeling petty, I held my hand up in the air and shot a bird. Now that I knew there were cameras in here, I had no doubt in my mind that he was watching me at this very moment.

A couple of hours later, I heard keys jiggling, and then the bedroom door opened. I jumped up expecting Alexandur to walk through the door, but instead it was Hero bringing me a big plate of food.

"Where is he at?" I asked Hero.

"He has retired to his study for the rest of the day and asked not to be bothered."

Hero sat the tray of food down on the nightstand and turned and walked away.

I walked over to the tray of food to see what was on it. He must have ordered food from somewhere because the salad was in a plastic container. I picked the apple up off the tray then turned around and walked back to the corner where the couch was and sat back down. Irritated, I ate my apple and then laid across the couch to take a nap.

"Ms. Kenya, wake up." Somebody shook me softly. I groaned and then opened my eyes. Hero was standing in front of me with another damn tray of food.

"Alexandur said you must eat, or you will regret it."

I picked my iPhone up and looked at the time. It was almost eight at night. Hero walked over to the nightstand and placed the food tray down before leaving. My stomach growled loudly. I stood up and stretched my arms out before walking over to pick up the food from the tray. Salmon, broccoli, and quinoa was what my warden had sent for me to eat. Hungrily, I devoured my plate in five minutes and then drank the water bottle that came with it. After placing the empty plate back down on the food tray, I decided to try to call Alexandur. The phone only rang one time and then he sent me to the voicemail.

My man: Yes?

Me: Why are you not here?

My man: I am here. I am in my office.

Me: Prove it.

My man: attachment sent.

I opened the attachment, and it was a picture of Alexandur eating the same thing I had just eaten.

Me: This proves nothing. I told you I would not be with a cheater.

My man: I would never cheat on you, but you will be punished every time you break the rules.

Me: You need help. You have too much money not to have a psychiatrist or someone to lock your crazy ass up in the mental ward.

My man: As long as they lock you up with me, I will go.

Me: Spoken like a true psychopath. When will you let me out my cell?

My man: In eighteen more hours.

I read and reread the message twice before calling his phone back. He was out of his mind if he thought he was about to lock me in this room for a full forty hours.

Me: If I am not out of here in the morning, I will tear up every expensive item of clothing you have in your closet with my bare hands.

My man: I'm a billionaire, it will all be replaced within the same hour, but you will get an extra day added on to your punishment for misbehaving.

Me: I hate you.

Upset, I got up from the couch and stomped into the bathroom to run me a bath. After my bath, I did the only other thing I could do and climbed my ass into the bed and went back to sleep.

Alexandur

Like a moth to a flame, as soon as the forty-eight hours was up, I was standing in front of my bedroom door. For the last two days, I have done nothing but watch Kenya on the cameras, but it wasn't enough. The time we spent apart caused me physical pain. I reached into my pocket and pulled the keys out and unlocked the door. A plate came flying at my head, but I ducked right before it could hit me. If I did not need to be in her space so badly, I would have closed the door back and added another forty-eight hours to her punishment. Unfortunately, Kenya was my weakness, and I could stay away no longer.

"Are you ready to talk now?" I asked her as I entered our bedroom. Kenya was sitting on the couch, looking out the window, trying to avoid my gaze. I went and sat right beside her on the couch.

"Do I have a choice, Alexandur?"

"No, you don't. Did you miss me?"

"Like I missed stubbing my big toe."

I chuckled and inhaled deeply, breathing in her air.

"What are the rules, Kenya?"

"I can't leave you and I have to stay out of other men's faces."

"If you know the rules, then why did you try to break them again? What did I do?" I asked, genuinely confused.

"You act like you don't really want me here."

Her answer stunned me. I thought I had been supportive and understanding. Was I still failing her miserably?

"What are you talking about? Elaborate. I need to know what made you feel that way exactly so I can fix the problem."

She got quiet and nibbled on her bottom lip before shrugging.

"We haven't had sex ever since you found out about my diagnosis," she whispered.

I stared at her while I gathered my thoughts. She was right, we had not had sex, but it was because of whatever bullshit she was feeding her brain.

"The reason we have not had sex has nothing to do with me not wanting you or wanting you here. That is ludicrous."

"Well, what's the reason then, Dr. Evil?"

I exhaled and shifted in the chair. Admitting my shortcomings as a man was not a conversation I wanted to have.

"I have not earned the right to have sex with you. It was my fault that you ended up in the hospital. If I had been paying attention to my woman as I should have, I would have known something was wrong. I failed my duties as your man and deserve to be punished, even if I have to punish myself."

Kenya's eyes widened and her mouth dropped open.

"You really believe that?" she asked me.

I nodded my head yes in confirmation. The facts were the facts, I messed up.

"Alexandur, you are blaming yourself for things that happened out of your control. You did not know about my diagnosis because I hid it. I had a flare-up because I have lupus and flare-ups happen. That was not my first time being hospitalized and it probably won't be my last. I know you like to run around town killing people like an antihero, but you are human. You can't control everything."

"You should be mad at me. You are too understanding."

"Naw, you just crazy as hell. Next time you want to punish yourself over things you cannot control, do not include me in the punishment. You putting me on dick punishment because you wanted to punish yourself is diabolical. I honestly thought you were about to do me like my ex did when he found out about my diagnosis."

Kenya laughed, but I did not find the humor.

"Do you want me to kill him?"

"Lord Jesus, please be a saint. No, Alexandur, I do not want you to kill him."

Kenya smiled at me brightly, and my heart sped up. I had the prettiest woman in the world and if anybody felt differently, they could die.

"I want to eat my pussy. Get naked."

Kenya's smile dropped and her eyes got low with lust. I licked my lips, my mouth ready to suck all the juice out of her pussy and then drink it to satisfy my thirst. Kenya stood up and started removing her clothes in front of me. I decided I want her to smother me with her pussy, so I stood up and went and laid across the bed.

"Come sit on my face now," I demanded. My dick was swollen and straining against my pants, ready to get out. Kenya took her time walking over to the bed and climbing over my face. If I weren't scared that my monster would hurt her, she would have paid for making me wait so long to dine. Hesitantly, she lowered her pussy down on my face. I grabbed hold of her hips and held her down so I could feast how I wanted to.

"Oh fuck," Kenya moaned. One of the things I loved about Kenya was how wet her pussy got. She was wetting my face up and I loved every moment of it. I sucked her clit into my mouth and bit down on it softly. She gasped and wiggled on top of me. My tongue flicked up and down on her clit repeatedly until she tried to run from my tongue. I stopped licking her clit to lift her up slightly and fuss.

"Stop running and grind that pussy on my face until I die."

This time when I lowered her back down on my face, I shoved my tongue deep inside of her pussy. Slowly, she been to grind on my face as if it was my dick. I was in heaven. My tongue moved in and out of her pussy until I could feel her pussy wall tightening up. I slid my tongue out of her pussy and sucked her clit back into my mouth.

"Baby, I'm about to cum," she moaned and then erupted. I held her down so her pussy juices could go all over my face. I wanted it in my eyes, in my nose, and in my mouth. She climbed off my face still huffing and puffing from the orgasm she just had.

"Pull my dick out and ride it until I nut."

She wasted no time following directions. I heard my zipper and felt her hands slide into my briefs. She pulled my dick out and spit on him.

"You know I like that nasty shit," I moaned. I thought she was about to climb on top of me but instead, she shoved my dick down her throat. The pleasure was so intense my toes curled. I grabbed a handful of her hair and pushed her face up and down. I was trying my best to be as gentle as possible with her, but she was begging my monster to come out to play. My eyes closed and I had to mentally make myself pull her hot, wet ass mouth off me.

"Ride my dick like I told you to do."

This time she complied. She positioned herself on top of me and slid her pussy down my dick.

"FUCK," I moaned. Kenya had the kind of pussy that would make a man start a war with Putin, Kim Jong Un, and Hitler's dead ass too.

"Choke me."

Kenya stopped grinding on my dick to look down at me. I glared at her, daring her to defy me. She nodded her head and wrapped her arms around my neck.

"Squeeze tighter." She tightened her hands around my neck and my nut rushed from my balls toward my dick. My hand went in between her legs to rub on her clit.

"Shit," she whispered. She stopped grinding and put her feet flat on the bed to bounce up and down on my dick.

My eyes rolled to the back of my head. I rubbed on her clit faster and then sprayed my nut all inside her deadly ass pussy.

"Yesssss!" Kenya screamed and came all over my dick while shaking.

Kenya

I thought when we had our conversation that any issues Alexandur was feeling inside were resolved. A week later, I realized that I thought wrong. Alexandur was still treating me with kid gloves. The man barely let me walk down the stairs by myself. He literally picked me up bridal style, of course, and carried me around like I was handicapped. We have only had sex one more time since our talk and he was being gentle again. I never thought the day would come when I wished my man would just slut me out, but as I pulled up the calendar on my phone, the day was here. It's really Alexandur's fault, because before I met him, I was used to having regular vanilla sex. Then he came into my life dicking me down and beating me up in the bedroom, now I can't go back to the old regular vanilla. That is why I am here with him now standing in a place I promised myself I would never go in. The idea of piercing my skin for a tattoo used to be an immediate no, but if it takes me getting a tattoo to show this man I am not a delicate flower, then so be it.

"Sotie, you ready?"

"As ready as I would ever be."

He chuckled and helped me climb onto the tattoo chair. The man tattooing us did all of Alexandur and his brothers' tattoos.

All Alexandur had to do was tell him that I was getting the eagle on my neck, and he knew what he was talking about.

"When she gets done, I want a letter put on all five of my knuckles."

"No problem, man, which hand are you getting tatted?"

"My right hand. I want the letters to spell out K-E-N-Y-A."

My mouth dropped open, and I stared at Alexandur in shock.

I hope you don't think this is a couple thing. I agreed to an eagle, that's it, that's all.

"I gotcha, man. Do you want me to put your name on the miss after I finish her eagle?"

"That will be a no," I answered for Alexandur.

"It doesn't matter to me either way, but I am curious, why not?"

I held up my left hand.

"Do you see a ring on my finger, specifically this finger?"

I wiggled my ring finger to make sure he knew which one I was talking about.

"Are you saying that after we get married, you'll get my name tattooed on you?" he asked me.

"Perhaps, let's get through the marriage part first and we will see."

Alexandur chuckled and then told me to sit back. I wanted to ask him to hold my hand, but the whole point of this was to show him that I could take a little pain.

Five minutes later, I was failing my mission miserably. Whoever said getting a tattoo didn't hurt needed they ass whoop. Alexandur told me it was a mind thing and that I had to blackout the buzzing noise of the tattoo gun because it triggered my brain to believe I was in pain when I really wasn't in pain. That was a whole bunch of reverse psychology bullshit. Alexandur was a liar and regardless of if I mentally blocked out the buzzing sound the tattoo gun made, I would still feel the pain physically.

"Can you hold my hand?" I asked Alexandur after ten more minutes passed by. I was sweating from the top of my head to the bottom of my feet. Alexandur reached his hand out and I grabbed it as tight as I could. He didn't even flinch. We stayed like that until it was time for the tattoo man to shade my tattoo. I liked to jump out of my seat. Getting my tattoo shaded had me crying and praying at the same time. When the man finally finished the whole tattoo, I promised myself I would never get another one.

Alexandur sat down in the tattoo chair after the tattoo man wiped the chair down.

"Give me a second to clean my tools and we can get it done. Is there a certain font size you want to use?" he asked Alexandur.

"No, you can just freestyle it," he replied.

Freestyling? What's that?

Alexandur's tattoo didn't take long at all. Within ten minutes, the man was done and Alexandur was handing him his card. Alexandur's phone rang while the man swiped his card on the card machine. I watched the tattoo man closely while he swiped because Atlanta was the home of scammers. When he finished, he tried to hand Alexandur his card back, but Alexandur was frozen with the phone to his ear.

"Baby, what's wrong?" I asked him. My heart dropped and I could tell from the expression on Alexandur's face that whatever it was wasn't good.

"Baby," I tried calling him again.

I gave up and reached to take the phone from him.

"Hey, who is this?"

"I've been shot, and our father has been killed. Y'all two get over to my house now," Constatin stated. In the background, you could hear Alexandur's mother crying loudly. I hung up the phone and slid it in my pocket.

"Oh my god," I gasped before grabbing Alexandur's hand and dragging him out of the tattoo shop.

"Baby, give me the keys," I told him as we approached his vehicle. Over the last few weeks, Alexandur had taken me over Constatin's house enough times for me to make it there without needing directions.

Alexandur reached into his pocket and slid the car keys out. He handed me the keys and we both jumped into his car.

"I am so, so sorry baby," I told Alexandur, and I truly was from the bottom of my heart. I knew how it felt to lose a parent suddenly and it sucked. I reached my right hand out and grabbed Alexandur's left hand. I drove the whole way to Constatin's house with one hand on the steering wheel and the other hand holding my man's hand tight.

When we pulled up to Constatin's house, I parked the car.

"Baby, please look at me."

Alexandur turned his face toward mine and I reached out to grab his face in my hand. We stared each other in the face while breathing in each other's breath. A minute later, I placed a kiss on his lips and then let his face go.

Alexandur stared at me for a few seconds and then nodded his head. We didn't have to say words to each other to understand that no matter what happened, he got me and I got him.

Alexandur

I've been shot and Father has been killed. I repeated the words over and over in my mind. Kenya and I had just spent the whole day at my parents' house yesterday and now I was being told my father was gone. Kenya pulled into my brother's house and called my name. She joined our faces together and we breathed. Every time I inhaled, I felt her energy enter my body. By the time she let my face go, I felt more in control. I got out of the car and walked around to the driver's side to open the door for Kenya. She got out and I reached down to join our hands together. When I walked into my brother's home, Roman was holding Mama. She was heaving and sobbing into his chest. Mentally, I knew I wasn't ready to address Mama yet. Roman caught my eyes and gone was his stone-faced expression. In its place was pure rage. My little brother was ready to kill somebody and I couldn't wait to figure out who. I continued walking until I reached Constatin's sitting room. There was only him, Kofi, and a doctor in the room. Constatin sat in his recliner with a glass cup full of brown liquor in his hand. My eyes roamed his body until they stopped at his knee. My monster started to stir inside, ready to kill at any moment. Kenya and I went to the couch that Kofi was sitting on and had a seat.

"Start at the beginning," I told my brother. I laid my head back against his couch and closed my eyes. Patiently, I waited on my brother to tell me who was about to die.

"I was at the office working when Father called me and told me to come to the house for a meeting. When I got to the house, I found out that Father had also invited Elizabeth to the house. She was sitting in his office chatting with him like she was already his daughter-in-law. Confused, I asked Father why he had called a meeting and what did Elizabeth have to do with it. Elizabeth had called Father and told him that she did not believe I would commit to her because I refused to talk about the wedding or start working on an heir right now. Angrily, I sat down and told Father that she was lying. Elizabeth appeared to be shocked and to be honest, she probably was because normally I would sit there and let her do whatever it was that she fucking wanted. Father took her side and told me I had a responsibility to uphold and unless I had a replacement ready to marry me and have an heir, then I needed to man up and make him proud. My iPhone rang and I ignored it. My iPhone rang again, and Father told me to see who it was. When I looked, it was Kofi. Confused, I didn't remember making any plans with him, so I answered the phone to see what was wrong. Kofi said he knew who had betrayed us. I sat up in the office chair and asked him who it was. Kofi said Elizabeth and Tom. I repeated their names, thinking he had to have made a mistake, when out of nowhere Elizabeth pulled a gun out of her purse and shot me in the knee and then Father in the head. She ran out of there and I tried my best to stand up to walk to Father. Three more shots rang out and everything got quiet. A few minutes later, Mama came running in the room shaken up and crying. Tom was with her when he spotted Elizabeth running out of the house. A guard reached for his gun to kill her, and he demanded the guards to stand down. All of them listened instead of Nick. Nick pulled his gun out anyway and Tom killed him. Mama said he ran out the house behind Liz, mumbling about how his plans were ruined and they had been planning this shit for almost a year."

"Elizabeth, your best friend, and Tom, the man who has been the head of our security for over ten years, were plotting to take us out?"

"Yes," he replied.

"Kofi, how did you figure it out?"

"Tom used the Swiss bank account as expected. I was able to follow the breadcrumbs back to the security firm. I broke into the security firm database and searched for any red flags. At first, I couldn't figure out who had double-crossed y'all until the day we were all at the hospital with Kenya. Constatin's phone rang and he stepped outside. Tom, unaware that he was being watched, looked at you like he wanted to kill you. That was strange to me because I hadn't heard anything about you and him having problems, but I also am new to the family, so what did I know? I tried to brush it off, but days had passed by and it was still bothering me. I asked to spend the weekend at your house again so that I could hack into your bodyguard Uno's phone. He is bad about sitting his phone down unsupervised to run his mouth. I got Tom's number out his phone and sent a phish text message from Uno's phone about mercenaries. He clicked on the email, and it gave me access to everything he did on his phone. The last problem was figuring out the other person with whom he was working. The person used a burner phone and for the most part, they only talked in code about how they couldn't want to take over and be together. Elizabeth slipped, though, when she texted and said she was coming to your parents' home to force Constatin to get her pregnant. I did not see the message right away because I was in school, but when I did figure it out, I asked to go to the bathroom and called Constatin."

"Why though? What was the endgame?"

"Power and revenge. Elizabeth wanted revenge on your brother because she was in love with him, and he didn't feel the same way about her. Tom was tired of working for other powerful people and was willing to do whatever it took to become a person of power. Once I figured out who they were, it was easier to decode their text messages to each other. Their plan was for Constatin to get her pregnant and marry her. They would then kill all of you and because she carried the only heir, she would step up and claim it was her rightful place to become Nasu. She would then marry Tom and step back while he did whatever he wanted."

"Thank you, Kofi. The million dollars will be deposited in your and Kenya's bank account within an hour. As of right now, your job remains the same. If they think they can run and hide from us, they are sorely mistaken."

"Cool, thanks bro. Please accept my condolences for you and your family."

"It is accepted."

Constatin was quiet the whole time while Kofi explained the missing puzzle pieces. The family doctor was now stitching his knee up, but Constatin's mind was elsewhere.

"Brother, you know to expect a call soon."

Constatin scoffed before taking a big sip of his liquor.

"They called me right before you got here. I am now the Nasu of the Romanian Mafia; well, if I complete the requirements in the time given."

My brother had been preparing for this role his whole life, but none of us thought he would get it by the death of our father.

"Let's go," I said to Kenya and stood. Tonight, I would drown my sorrows in a bottle of the strongest liquor I had in my office, and tomorrow I would complete my duties as the son of the former Nasu. On the way out of the door, I grabbed my mama out of Roman's arm and held her tight.

"Go take some sleep medicine and get some rest, Mama."

I placed a kiss on her forehead and walked out.

Kenya

Alexandur's father had more security at his funeral than the president had security at the White House. I guess that is to be expected when the funeral was full of Mafia families. The funeral took place at a graveside instead of in a church like I was used to. Only immediate family was allowed to stand on the front row. There was Constatin, their mama, me, Alexandur, Roman, and then Kofi. Alexandur told me that we were not allowed to show any emotion because it would be a sign of weakness to the other Mafia families. So together we stood in unity. If a person would have told me three months ago that I would fall in love with a capo of the Romanian Mafia, I would have told them to leave that dope alone. Yet here I was, very much in love and dare I say happy. Alexandur was not a good man, but he never portrayed himself to be. He was what he was, and I am the woman who is going to stand right beside him through it all. At the end of the funeral, it was Romanian custom to light incense and place wine in and around the coffin.

Because there were so many dangerous individuals in one spot, Constatin had decided against inviting people over to the family house for a gathering. When the funeral ended, we went back to Alexandur's mama's house and made sure she ate and was in bed resting before we left. Roman was staying there with her along with security to make sure she was safe. By the time we got home, I was exhausted. I told Alexandur I was going upstairs to shower and rest a little as soon as we walked through the door. He nodded his head and went in the opposite direction. For the last few days, Alexandur had been spending all his time in his office drinking himself into a stupor. I respected his way of grieving, but after today, I planned on telling him that he needed to find a healthier way to cope.

I showered and got into the bed to take a nap.

"Kenya, you better wake up. Your man is downstairs acting like a madman. I told him that I personally checked Tree and Hero out and they had nothing to do with Tom's betrayal. He is not listening to logic."

Kofi was standing beside the bed shaking my body, trying to wake me up.

"He is doing what?" I asked my brother drowsily.

"About to kill his bodyguards if you don't get your ass up."

My eyes shot open, and I jumped out the bed. Kofi ran down the stairs to the kitchen. I followed right behind him.

Lord Jesus.

Alexandur was pacing back and forth, mumbling to himself about all rats must die while swinging a big ass butcher knife in his hand.

Tree and Hero were tied up to chairs. He had beaten them so badly I could barely recognize the difference between the two.

"Alexandur, you must have lost your motherfucking mind. If you don't put that fucking knife down and let them the fuck go right now!" I yelled.

He stopped pacing and looked up at me with a smile on his face. His eyes were pitch black and I knew my monster had come out to play.

"No. Go back upstairs."

Alexandur stopped pacing and took the knife and cut Tree

down the side of his face with it. He then leaned in and licked the damn blood dripping from the cut.

"Oh hell naw, that motherfucker is psychotic as fuck. Let me go mind my happy-to-be-alive ass business," Kofi stated.

Alexandur lifted the knife and stabbed Hero in his arm. That was it, I had seen enough. If I didn't do something quick, he was going to kill them.

"You are such a little bitch!" I yelled at him.

Kofi looked at me like I had lost my mind.

"Girl, do you see what I see? If you don't shut the fuck up," he whispered to me.

"Awwww, look at the big bad monster scared to come after the person he really wants. I'm the one you want to hurt, you just a scary little bitch," I taunted him.

For the first time since I met him, Alexandur burst out into full laughter. He put the knife down on the table and then turned his head to the side to look at me.

"Kofi, I know this looks crazy, but I need you to trust me. Alexandur won't hurt me like that. When we go upstairs, untie them, and take them to the hospital."

"What you mean, he won't hurt you like that? The fuck kind of crazy shit y'all got going on?"

"Just do as I say, Kofi!" I demanded.

Alexandur and I stared each other down.

"Kenya. RUN!" Alexandur ordered, and I took off running back toward the stairs.

Fear and excitement had my panties soaked before I reached the top of the stairs. The first place Alexandur looked would be our bedroom, so I ran toward his office. I twisted the doorknob and it was unlocked. There weren't many places to hide inside his office. I had to decide between his office bathroom and under his desk. Quickly, I ran to his desk, moved the desk chair back, and climbed under it.

Silently, I prayed Kofi listened and went to take Tree and Hero to get the medical attention they needed.

"Come out, come out, wherever you are," Alexandur sang in the hallway. My heart started beating faster. If Alexandur took one look at my shorts, he would see the wet spot that now stained them and know how turned on I was.

The office door opened and I held my breath, hoping he couldn't hear me breathing.

"Ahhhhhh!" I screamed. Alexandur grabbed a handful of my hair and pulled me from under his office desk.

He threw me against the wall in his office and then watched as my body hit the floor. My body slightly ached, but that didn't stop me from jumping up and trying to make a run for the door. He caught me by my hair again and dragged me back to him. Alexandur put his face in my neck and sniffed.

"I want to hurt you, Kenya," he whispered in my ear.

"There goes my monster. I thought for a minute that you had turned into a little bitch baby," I taunted him. I needed him to see that I could still handle his monster. Hell, I craved his monster.

"Get on your knees. I want to choke you with my dick," he growled out lowly into my ear.

I fell to my knees in front of him and unzipped his pants. My hands reached inside his briefs and pulled his dick out. Slowly, I jacked his dick up and down before reaching down to gently grab his balls.

"Spit on it," he demanded.

I gathered as much spit as I could in my mouth and spit on the top of his dick. He groaned before grabbing my hair and shoving his dick down my throat. I gagged and tears fell down my face.

"Put your finger in my ass."

My right hand went in between his legs and to his ass. I slid my index finger up and down his ass crack before plunging my finger deep inside him.

Alexandur moaned loudly and it almost made me cum. Hearing him moan was intoxicating to me. It made my pussy wetter every time he verbally expressed how much I was pleasing his body. My finger slid in and out of his ass while his dick slid in and out of my mouth.

"Shit. Swallow it all. You better not waste a single drop."

Alexandur shoved his dick down my throat one last time and held my head so that I couldn't move. His nut shot down my throat, and like the good little slut I am, I swallowed every drop of it.

"Fuck, that felt good, but I need to hear you scream. Go bend over my desk. I am ramming my dick inside of your virgin asshole tonight."

"Don't you need lube for that?" I asked him. He snatched me up by my hair and tossed me on his desk. I felt his hands grab a handful of my ass checks before he pulled my shorts and panties down in one shove. My hands grabbed the edge of his desk tight. I had heard stories about how painful anal sex was the first time, and that was with lubrication being applied. Alexandur spread my ass checks apart and I felt the head of his dick pushing against my virgin asshole. He had to push a few times before he was able to slide one inch of his dick inside my ass, and it burned like hell.

"Alexandur, there is no way in the world your whole dick is fitting inside of my ass," I told him while shaking my head. If one inch felt like this then I didn't want to find out what eight inches felt like.

"Kenya, hold on the edge of the desk tight."

Alexandur grabbed a hold of my hips and then thrust his whole dick in my ass. Pain struck through my body so intensely that I screamed.

"Good girl. Fuck, sotie, I am not going to last long in this tight asshole."

Alexandur reached around the front of my body until he reached my pussy and started rubbing on my clit. The pain I was feeling in my body started to turn into pleasure after a few minutes.

"That's it, open up for me," he encouraged me.

He pushed my back down so that my body laid all the way flat on his desk and increased the speed of his thrusts. I felt my body tighten up and an orgasm started to build.

"I love you," I moaned. It was my first time admitting how I felt about him out loud and I instantly felt relief once I did it.

This orgasm felt different, more powerful than any I had ever felt before. My body began trembling and I swear I could see stars in my eyes. A scream tore from my throat and my body erupted into a million pieces. Alexandur bit down on the back of my neck and then growled. His nut filled my asshole up. It was so much that it was dripping out of my asshole and down my leg.

"Thank you," he whispered in my ear, before sliding his dick out of my ass.

"It is going to hurt for you to try to walk right now. I am going to carry you to our bed to wait while I run your bath."

I nodded my head weakly. Alexandur bent down and scooped me in his arms.

"Four weeks, Kenya. You have four weeks to plan the wedding you want."

I frowned and then looked him in his eyes.

"Are you joking or being serious, Alexandur?"

"I am being very serious. I love you with every fiber of my dark soul. You have four weeks and not a day more before we make this official."

Kenya

The wedding

Today was the day I married the love of my life, and I was so nervous. The last four weeks have been a struggle, to say the least. Thank God I had Alexandur's mama to help me. She had done most of the wedding planning and all I had to do was say yes or no. In a way, I think it helped her because she had something to focus on to keep her from falling into a deep depression over the loss of her beloved husband.

Kofi was giving me away today. He was so happy when I asked him, even though he asked me if I was sure that I wanted to marry Alexandur's psycho ass. I told him there wasn't anybody else on this earth more perfect for me than Alexandur. We were created for one another.

I glanced at myself in the mirror one more time. My wedding dress was black instead of white. A black wedding gown symbolized loyalty to my husband until death did us part. Plus, there was nothing pure and innocent about the man I was about to marry, and I wasn't about to pretend that there was. The black wedding dress I selected was shoulderless and backless. It had a deep V-cut around the bodice area, and the skirt of the dress flared out dramatically like the ballgown dresses kids wore to prom. My hair had been flat ironed straight and I went with a middle part because I wanted to bring attention to my face. The makeup artist I hired had magical hands. She did a natural beat with a smoky-eye look to match my dress.

"Damn. I was looking for my best friend, but it seems I have stumbled into a supermodel's dressing room. I apologize," I heard a female voice say.

I turned away from the mirror very fast and speed-walked to the dressing room door where Ari stood smiling. She held her arms open wide for me, and I went right into them.

"You told me that you couldn't make it!" I whined.

"Girl, your husband wanted to surprise you. You were crazy to believe that I would miss your wedding day anyway," she laughed.

God, I had missed my best friend so much. I wrapped my arms around her tightly.

"You better not start crying, Kenya. I am here to stay for good now."

"What do you mean?" I asked her, confused.

"I found a nursing job here in Atlanta," she replied.

Today was indeed the happiest day of my life. I was about to marry my monster, he was signing Hooters over to me before we went on our honeymoon, and my best friend was moving to Atlanta. I didn't know what I did to deserve so many blessings, but I silently thanked God before the music started playing in the background, signaling the start of my wedding.

Alexandur

The music began playing, signaling the start of my wedding. All day I had been praying that Kenya wouldn't decide I was too dark for her and try to run. I would have found her and brought her back, but that was beside the point. Constatin was my best man. I watched as he walked down the aisle. He still had a slight limp and had to use a cane to walk around, but somehow it only made him appear more powerful instead of weak. Roman was the next one to walk out. He had his signature bland look on his face as he walked down the aisle. I had been worried about him. Since Father's death, he has had something sinister brewing inside of him. Something even more sinister than the monster I had inside of me. The music changed and the opera song I selected began playing. Confidently, I strolled down the aisle, head held high, to stand in my appointed spot. It wasn't until I reached my spot and turned toward all the people in the crowd that my heart started racing. The music changed again, and I held my breath until I saw Kofi and my beautiful bride walking toward me. I had imagined a million times how Kenya would look today, and nothing I imagined came close to the breathtakingly beautiful woman headed my way. She had on a black wedding gown with a black veil covering her face.

It seemed like time slowed and everybody disappeared as I waited on my *sotie* to stand before me. When she finally made it to me, I reached over to pull the black veil from Kenya's face. I grabbed her by her neck and kissed her passionately. In the background, I heard my oldest brother clearing his throat, but he and everybody else could wait.

Twenty-five minutes later it was official. Kenya had married the monster, and I would never let her go.

Epilogue
Constatin

The mind was what my father called me. I was supposed to be the smart one, the one who figured everything out. Where the fuck was my mind when my best friend was plotting against me? Where the fuck was my mind when the head of our security was planning on killing us? I took a sip of my liquor before glancing around at my brother's wedding. Everybody was on the dance floor having a good time. I had even seen my mama smile once or twice today. On the outside looking in, one would assume I was handling everything going on in my normal cool, calculated way. My brothers and I were taught at an early age how to conceal our true emotions from showing on our face. So although I may have outwardly appeared calm, cool, and in control, I was really boiling with rage inside.

All day I could feel people's eyes on me, and it was what was to be expected as the Nasu. My brother had some of the biggest Mafia families in attendance today and I know they all wondered what my next move would be. The people I trusted the most had betrayed me in the worst way, and I had to set an example that would be remembered for generations to come. Before I could plot my revenge though, I needed to get married and fast. I was only given sixty days to find a new bride, and thirty of those days had already passed. To be honest, it didn't matter to me who I married. The marriage would be a business transaction for me and nothing more. My eyes went back to the dance floor, and I saw my brother's new wife Kenya dancing with her best friend. I believe her name was Ari. They were polar opposites of each other. Kenya was taller than her and slim with a dark-chocolate skin complexion. Her best friend couldn't be more than five feet tall, she had what my mama called baby-making hips, and her skin complexion was milk chocolate.

"Fiul," my mama called out to me from the dance floor. She wanted me to come dance with her, but there was no way I was going out there on the dance floor with his aggravating ass cane. I had two more weeks of physical therapy before I could ditch it. The doctor said that I would always walk with a slight limp, but eventually, it would be barely noticeable. Flashbacks of my best friend shooting a bullet through my knee appeared in my mind again. Elizabeth was smart to run and hide. She knew like I knew that her days of being alive would be coming to an end soon.

An hour later, I stood up from the table where I sat to wish my brother and his new wife farewell on their honeymoon. I grabbed my cane to walk to the bathroom to relieve my bladder. My security guards followed closely behind me. When I reached the bathroom, they went in before me to clear the bathroom stalls. Unfortunately, being the head of the Romanian Mafia came with having a lot of enemies known and unknown.

I leaned against the wall waiting on my security guards to finish the bathroom check when someone bumped into me from behind. My cane slipped out of my hands and onto the floor. I felt wet liquid on my suit jacket. I grabbed my gun from my waist and turned around.

"Oh my god! Please don't shoot me. Shit, y'all motherfuckers are crazy," Kenya's best friend said, before reaching down to pick up my cane.

"Here. My bad. Also, I accidentally spilled my cup on your

jacket. If you send me the bill from the cleaners, I will pay it," she said.

I turned my head to the side and stared at her.

"Um, excuse me, *Mr. Man With the Gun*, are you going to get your cane from my hand or continue looking at me crazy?"

She reached her hand out to hand me my cane again, but I didn't reach my hand out to get it from her.

"Sir, can you stop staring at me like that? It was an accident. I already apologized. What more do you want?"

Her voice was full of attitude, and I found it amusing.

"That's a good question, Ari. Because what I want, is your hand in marriage and a baby. Unfortunately for you, I am not giving you a choice in the matter."

To Be Continued...

To My Readers:

Thank you all so much. I appreciate each and every one of you. Please consider leaving me an honest review. It helps me out so much. I hope you all enjoyed the wild ride we had with Kenya and Alexandur. Roman and Ari story is up next and will be dropping soon. To stay informed on all projects and sneak peeks, follow me on Facebook:Author Jatoria Crews, and join my authors group, Jatoria C. Book Cove. My IG, Tiktok, and Threads are all under Author Jatoria Crews. All of this information above can be found on my website:www.author-jatoriac.com. Thank you again for the support.

Also by Jatoria C.

Obsessed With A Plus Size Barbie 3
Obsessed With A Plus Size Barbie 2
Obsessed With A Plus Size Barbie
Alexa, Play I Need A Rich Thug Husband 2
Alexa, Play I Need A Rich Thug Husband

Printed in Great Britain
by Amazon